## Praise for the work of Ron Arias:

"Be prepared to be astonished by Arias's storytelling and his world of youthful adventures where the imagination meets real-world knowledge. He writes of families disrupted by personal tragedy and war that manage to survive, of a community where young and old come to each other's assistance."
—Héctor Enrique Calderón Valle, Professor of Spanish,
University of California, Los Angeles

"*The Road to Tamazunchale* is one of the first achieved works of Chicano consciousness and spirit."                                      —*Library Journal*

"In terms of craftsmanship and artistry no Chicano novel before *The Road to Tamazunchale* has tapped the artistic resources of the modern and contemporary novel (and the arts) in a comparable way, deliberately and intuitively . . . daring and commendable."
—*Latin American Literary Review*

"Arias, who reported the story in *People* magazine, here interviews virtually everybody involved in this affair, and reconstructs the agony of the families waiting at home as well as the desperation of the fishermen. The account of their adjustment to their plight is as interesting as the fact of their survival."
—*Publishers Weekly* on *Five Against the Sea*

# *The*
# Wetback
## *and Other Stories*

## RON ARIAS

Arte Público Press
Houston, Texas

*The Wetback and Other Stories* is funded in part by a grant from the City of Houston through the Houston Arts Alliance.

*Recovering the past, creating the future*

Arte Público Press
University of Houston
4902 Gulf Fwy, Bldg 19, Rm 100
Houston, Texas 77204-2004

Cover design by Caroline McAllister
Cover image by Paul Botello

Names: Arias, Ron, 1941- author.
Title: The wetback : and other stories / by Ron Arias.
Description: Houston, TX : Arte Publico Press, [2016]
Identifiers: LCCN 2016025128I ISBN 9781558858343
    (softcover : acid-free paper) I ISBN 9781518501005 (ePub) I
    ISBN 9781518501012 (kindle) I ISBN 9781518500992 (pdf)
Classification: LCC PS3551.R427 A6 2016 I DDC 813/.54—
    dc23 LC record available at https://lccn.loc.gov/2016025128

♾ The paper used in this publication meets the requirements of
the American National Standard for Information Sciences—
Permanence of Paper for Printed Library Materials, ANSI
Z39.48-1984.

16 17 18 19 20          7 6 5 4 3 2 1

# Table of Contents

# Author's Note

Most of these stories were written and published in the early 1970s when I was teaching and had the time and motivation to write creatively. I was driven to write fiction because I wanted to make sense of my life and life in general in my own way. And then for about thirty years I stopped writing about imaginary people and places, mainly because I had jumped into a rollercoaster of real-life stories as a journalist with a global beat, often feeling like a character in my own reported stories.

That period ended and I returned to writing fiction, motivated by the same business of making sense of people and what they do. Many of these tales may be read as allegories about a Los Angeles neighborhood called Frog Town, which no longer has an abundance of frogs and exists officially as Elysian Valley. But the stories all spring from actual facts, from a time when frogs were everywhere, when children found a drowned man in a dry riverbed or when a young soldier went off to war, disappeared and became myth.

For this collection, I have sharpened or rewritten published stories and have written two new pieces.

*To Joan*

# The Wetback

That afternoon, Mrs. Rentería's neighbor's grandchildren discovered David in the dry riverbed. The young man was absolutely dead, the children could see that. For a long time they watched him from behind the clump of cat-o'-nine-tails. His body lay so still that even a mouse, poking into one nostril, suspected nothing. The girl approached first, leaving behind her two brothers. David's brow was smooth; his gray-blue eyes were half closed; his dark skin glistened, clean and wet, and the rest of him, torn shirt and patched trousers, was also wet.

"He drowned," the girl said.

The boys ran over for their first good look at a dead man. David was more or less what they expected, except for the gold tooth in front and a mole beneath one sideburn. His name wasn't David yet; that would come later when the others found out. David was the name of a boy who drowned years ago when Cuca predicted it wouldn't rain and it did and the Los Angeles River overflowed, taking little David to the bottom or to the sea, no one knew, because all they found was a washtub he used as a boat.

Circling the body, the older brother said, "How could he drown? There's no water."

"He did," the girl said. "Look at him."

The younger boy backed away. "I'm telling."

The brothers then ran across the dry sand pebbles, up the concrete bank and disappeared behind the levee. Before the crowd of neighbors arrived, the girl wiped the dead man's face with her skirt hem, straightened his clothes as best she could and tried to remove the sand in his hair. She raised David's head, made a claw with her free hand and raked over the black hair. His skull was smooth on top, with a few bumps above the nape. Finally she made a part on the right side, then sat down on the sand with the young man's head on her lap.

Tiburcio and the boys were the first to reach her, followed by the fishmonger Smaldino and the other men. Most of the women waited on the levee until Tiburcio signaled it was okay, the man was dead. Carmela, the youngest of the women, helped Mrs. Rentería first, since it was her neighbor's grandchildren who had discovered David. Then she gave a hand to the other older women.

For some time they debated the cause of death. No bruises, no bleeding, only a slight puffiness to the skin, especially the hands. Someone said they should remove the shoes and socks.

"No," Tiburcio said. "Leave him alone, he's been through enough. Next you'll want to take off his clothes."

Tiburcio was overruled: off came the shoes, a little water and sand spilling out. Both socks had holes at the heels and big toes.

"What about the pants?" the grocer Wong asked. "You going to leave them all wet and sandy?"

"All right, let's take them off," Tiburcio said, rolling his eyes back, seemingly resigned to the inevitable.

In this way they discovered the man not only lacked a small toe on one foot but also had a large tick burrowed in his right thigh and a long scar running from one hip almost to the navel.

"Satisfied?" Tiburcio asked the crowd.

Everyone was silent.

David was certainly the best looking young man they had ever seen, at least naked as he now lay. No one seemed to have the slightest shame before this perfect shape of a man. It was as if a statue had been placed among them and they stared freely at whatever they admired most. Some of the men envied the wide chest, the angular jaw or the hair, thick and wavy. The women for the most part gazed at the full, parted lips, the sun-baked arms, the long, strong legs, and of course the dark, soft mound with its finger of life flopped over, its head to the sky.

"Too bad about the missing toe," Wong said.

Smaldino elbowed his way forward for closer scrutiny. "And the tick, what about that?" he said after a moment's inspection.

Mrs. Rentería asked for a book of matches, which Wong quickly gave her. After striking the match head on the cover, she held the tiny flame close to the engorged, whitish sac until the insect withdrew. There were oohs and ahs, and the girl who had combed the dead man's hair began to cry. Carmela glanced at the levee, wondering what was keeping her uncle Fausto.

They all agreed it was death by drowning. That the river was dry occurred only to the children, but they remained quiet, listening to their parents continue about what should be done with the dead man. Smaldino volunteered his ice locker. No, the women complained. He would lose his suppleness, the smooth, lifelike skin would turn blue and harden. Then someone suggested they take him to Cuca, perhaps she knew how to preserve the dead. Cuca had cures for everything, so why not for this beauty of a man?

"No!" Mrs. Rentería shouted, unable to control herself any longer. "He'll stay with me." Although she had never married, never been loved by a man, everyone called her Mrs. out of respect, at times even knowing the bite of irony could be felt in this small, squarish woman who surrounded her house with flowers and worked six days a week changing bedpans and sheets at County General. "David is mine!" she shouted defiantly.

"Who says?" Tiburcio asked. "And since when is his name David? He looks to me more like a . . . " Tiburcio glanced at the man's face. " . . . a Luis."

"No señor!" another voice cried. "Roberto."

"Antonio!"

"Henry."

"¡Qué Henry! Enrique!"

"Alex!"

Trini, Ronnie, Miguel, Roy, Rafael, Bruce Lee . . . The list grew, everyone shouting a name. One by one they turned away to debate the naming, everyone except Mrs. Rentería. She stepped next to her prize and kneeled for a moment. Then she stood and wrung out the sopping gray shorts. Gently, she slipped his feet through the holes in the pathetic garment, eventually tugging the elastic band past the knees to the thighs. Here she asked for help, but the group of curious adults and children didn't seem to hear. So with a determination grown strong by years of spinsterhood, she rolled the body onto one side, then the other, at last working the shorts up to his waist. The rest was the same and she finished dressing him by herself.

In the end, Mrs. Rentería had her way. When the others stopped arguing, they returned to surround the body, now clothed, although no one seemed to notice. He appeared as breathtaking dressed as he did naked. "You're right," Tiburcio told Mrs. Rentería, "his name is David . . . but you still can't have him."

About this time Fausto arrived, helped by Mario, a hip, goateed boy whose weaknesses were stealing cars and befriending old men. The two figures stepped slowly across the broken glass and rocks. Fausto, winking at his niece, immediately grasped the situation. David was a wetback. Yes, there was no mistake. Years ago, hadn't he brought at least a dozen young men from Tijuana, one, sometimes two at a time, cramped in the trunk of the car? Months later, after they had found work, the grateful fellows would sometimes show up at his house, dressed in new clothes, sometimes sporting an earring in one lobe. The clothes, even when spiffy, were always the same kind of clothes. Fausto wasn't too quick to spot the new women arrivals, but the men, like young David here, were an easy mark.

"How can you tell?" Smaldino asked.

The old man raised the hoe he used as a staff and pointed to the gold tooth, the cut of hair, the narrow trouser cuffs, the scuffed, pointy shoes. "It's all there. You think I don't know a *mojado* when I see one?" As a last gesture, he stooped down and closed the dead man's eyes. "Now, what will you do with him?"

A small girl stepped close to Fausto and asked if she could have the young man.

"No, *m'ijita*, he's too old for you."

Mrs. Rentería repeated her claim, and before the others could object, Fausto asked in a loud voice what woman among them needed a man so much that she would accept a dead man?

"Speak up! Which of you can give this man your entire love, the soul of everything you are? Which of you, if not the *señora* here? She has no one."

The wives looked at their husbands, and the girls and unmarried women and widows waited in silence.

"Then it's settled," Fausto said with unusual authority. "You, Tiburcio . . . and you, Smaldino, and you, Mario, take this man to her house."

"Hey, I ain't touchin' no dead man," Mario said.

Carmela stepped forward. "That figures. You go around stealing cars but you won't help us out here."

"All right, all right," Mario muttered, "one time and no more."

That evening so many visitors crowded into the small, frame house next to the river that latecomers were forced to wait their turn in the front yard. Even Cuca, her stockings rolled down to her ankles, had to wait in line.

Mrs. Rentería had bathed and shaved David, clipped his hair and lightly powdered his cheeks. He wore new clothes and sat quietly in a waxed and polished leather recliner. The neighbors filed by, each shaking the manicured hand, each with a word of greeting, some of the men with a joking remark about the first night with a woman. And most everyone returned for a second, third and fourth look at this treasure of manhood that might not survive another day of summer heat.

Like all discoveries, it was only a matter of time until David's usefulness for giving pleasure would end, until the colognes and sprays would not mask what was real, until the curious would remain outside, preferring to watch through the window with their noses covered, until the women retreated in the yard, until the men stopped driving by for a glance from the street, until at last only Mrs. Rentería was left to witness the end.

Happily this was a solitary business. For several days she had not gone to the hospital, her work was forgotten, and she passed the daylight hours at David's feet, listening, speaking, giving up secrets. And not once did he notice her splotchy hands, the graying hair nor the plain, uninspired face. During the warm afternoons David would take her out, arm in arm, to stroll through the lush gardens of his home, somewhere far away to the south. He fed her candies, gave her flowers and eventually spoke of eternity and a breeze that never dies. At night she would come to him dressed as a dream, a sprig of jasmine in her hair, then lie by his side until dawn, awake to his every whisper and touch.

On the third day Fausto knew the honeymoon was over. "Señora!" he called at the door. "It's time David left."

Mrs. Rentería hurried out from the kitchen. Her hair was down in a carefree tangle and she wore only a bathrobe. "You're too late," she said with a smile. "He died this morning . . . about an hour ago."

Fausto examined her eyes, quite dry and obviously sparkling with something more than grief.

"He died?"

"Yes," she said with a nod and a smile, "of love."

The odor of death was so strong Fausto had to back down the steps. "Señora, I'd be more than happy to take him away for you. Leave it to me. I'll be right back."

"Wait!" she shouted. "David's already gone."

"I know but I'll take him away."

"That's what I mean. The boy, that *greñudo* friend of yours, carried him off just before you came."

"Mario?"

"I think so. He's got *pelitos* on his chin."

"Then fine, señora. Your David will get the best burial ever."

Mrs. Rentería told Fausto she wanted to go with Mario but the young thief told her to stay home. He would take care of David's send-off himself.

"Don't worry," Fausto said, "we'll take good care of him. The body goes, but the soul . . . "

"I know, his soul is right here . . . in my heart."

"*Señora,* keep him there because if you ever lose him, watch out for the other women."

"He'll never leave. You see, I have his word." She pulled a folded scrap of paper from between her breasts and studied the scribbled words.

Fausto asked if he should say something special at the burial. "Some prayer . . . a poem?"

Mrs. Rentería answered with a toss of her head. For a moment, the glassy eyes were lost in the distance. Then she closed the heavy wooden door, clicked both locks, dropped the blinds behind the big, bay window and drew them shut.

David was not buried. "A man so perfect should not be buried," Fausto told Mario. With the teenager's help and using a skill more ancient than the first Tarahumara natives, the old man set to work in his backyard, painstakingly restoring David to his former self. Even the missing toe was replaced.

By late evening the restoration was complete. Only one chore remained. Carmela brought a pitcher of water into the yard and wet the dead man's clothes, the same shabby clothes he wore when he had arrived.

"More water," Fausto said.

Mario took the pitcher from Carmela's hands and skipped into the house. David was about his own age, heavier, but he could have been a brother. Ever since Mrs. Rentería had taken the dead stranger home, Mario's admiration for David's composure and quiet sense of confidence had grown. "The dude is cool," Mario now thought as he returned with the filled pitcher, "but he's got to leave Elysian Valley looking as fresh and wet as he was when he had arrived."

After David was doused a second time, Fausto asked for the egg—a dried quetzal egg Mario had plucked from the Museum of Natural History's ornithology collection.

"What's that for?" Carmela asked.

"Oh, Cuca once told me that you do this"—Fausto lightly brushed the egg on the dead man's lips—"and it brings him good luck. I don't believe it . . . but you know, just in case . . . can't hurt."

Fausto stood back and examined his work under the porch light. "Mario, pick him up."

"Hey, man, I thought it was over."

"Almost. Just do as I say."

Mario struggled with the body, lifting it over one shoulder.

"Follow me," Fausto said.

Carmela opened the picket-fence gate for her uncle and a burdened Mario. "Tío, where are you taking him?" she asked as they slowly crossed the street under a broken street lamp.

"Further down the river," came Fausto's faint reply, "where others can find him."

# Eddie

I don't think Eddie Vera had ever been in a fight he hadn't won. Badass wouldn't even apply. Maybe killer, or monster, or Godzilla. If you were smart, you made friends with him and he might have become your protector, which is what happened to me. That was back in seventh grade.

Eddie was a new kid too but the eighth- and ninth-graders already knew about him and left him alone. Only the *pachucas* went after undersized guys like me.

Initiation was something you just tried to forget was going to happen. All summer long you tried to push it away but you knew it was coming. The possibility sat in the back of your brain like a mud ball with a rock inside, hidden, ready to do you in the first day of classes. What the gangs and *clicas* didn't know was that Eddie's grandmother and my grandmother were *comadres*, and my *abuela* told his that he should watch out for me.

Also, Eddie and I had one thing in common that would bond us for life: we'd both lost our parents, his in a head-on car crash when he was six and mine at birth in Mexico when I was adopted by my "grandmother." I didn't hear about him protecting me until much later; Eddie himself would never have told me. If he did, he'd probably say it was no big deal, just one of his duties to even the odds.

So the first day after school these four *pachuquitas* came after me with switchblades, can openers and hairpins. I ran but they cornered me under the track bleachers, held me on the ground and pulled my pants off. Then a girl with her eyes made up like a cat's told me to take my shorts off. I was thinking, "I'd never do that." But she poked me in the butt with a hairpin and yelled, "Do it or I'll stick it all the way in."

I took off my shorts and covered myself with my hands. The girls laughed, and one of them told me I'd have to run around the track before they'd give me back my pants. But the girls weren't going to give me back my shorts, which they said they'd run up the school flagpole.

That's when Eddie showed up. He started kicking and swinging, knocking down Cat Girl before she could pull out her knife. He kicked another girl, knocking her to the ground. With this low growl, baring his teeth, he chomped down on another girl's arm, got her by her big hairdo and spun her around until she started screaming and begging for him to let her go. Then he went after Cat Girl. In those days *pachucas* wore everything tight, especially skirts, so they really couldn't run, which is what the Cat tried to do.

Eddie got to her right away, pushed her down again, and then made her crawl back to where I was by the bleachers.

"Say you're sorry," he said, "and I'll never bother you again."

She apologized, and they gave me back all my clothes. Then Eddie told them to leave so I could dress.

"Get outta here! And don't say nothin' about this. Understand? Or I'll get you, all of you, one by one."

After he rescued me, I never again had a problem. Same thing in high school. I saw plenty of fights but I never felt threatened, even after Eddie dropped out in his sophomore year.

We called him Super Cabrón, also Loco, Crazy and Trouble. He did time everywhere, even Soledad, for drugs, for dealing, for stealing cars, for armed robbery. When he got out of Soledad the last time, he looked skinnier than I'd ever seen him, hiding his tattoos with long-sleeve shirts and cutting his hair military style, not slicked-back anymore.

He got a job sanding cars in an auto body shop. For a few years he lived so straight and out of trouble that his parole officer became his best friend. I had moved away from the neighborhood but I still visited my grandmother's place on Blake. She told me she started seeing him in church, which surprised me. Then she told me Eddie had become a Republican, which surprised me even more.

Somebody must have convinced him it was the way to power, real power, not just street power. So when the campaign started, there was Eddie in a suit and tie going door-to-door, giving little speeches about his candidate and handing out campaign stuff. When he came around to my grandmother's house, I was sitting on the sofa watching the Spanish news about an assassination in El Salvador. Through the screen door I saw him open the little gate of the white picket fence and approach the house.

I got up and opened the door as he was coming up to the porch steps. "Hey, Eddie, that really you?"

"It's me."

"Man, what happened to you?"

"Whaddaya mean?" He looked surprised.

"I mean . . . well, you know . . . "

He cut me off, not with words but with that scary, hard look of his. "Read this," he said and held out a pamphlet with some guy's picture on the front. "He's a good man."

I took the pamphlet. Above the handsome, smiling face were the words GET GOING WITH AL GOMEZ. Under the photo were the equally large words ADELANTE CON AL GOMEZ. Eddie, a big man, looked down at me as I looked at the pamphlet. I didn't really read the inside but for a few moments pretended to check it out.

"Vote for him," Eddie said, almost commanding me.

"Yeah, man."

"Say hi to your grandma."

"I will. She's at the eye doctor's."

"How're you?"

"Can't complain."

"College?"

"Yeah, I made it through."

"Good," he said, nodding and turning to head down the steps. "Gotta move."

"Take care," I said. "*Cuídate*."

"Always do."

He never turned around, just pointed a finger into the air, saying something about always taking care of Number One. And that was the last time we spoke.

A few months later, after Eddie's candidate lost by a lot, I heard that he had joined the Army. He wasn't drafted like a lot of guys back then. He joined up after he heard some senator call for more volunteers to join the military, especially Spanish speakers. They were needed in Central America and other places.

Eddie would have liked that because Doña Mercedes, his grandmother, said he had come out at the top of his paratrooper class and was now off leading a patrol somewhere. Later, she told my grandmother she got postcards from Honduras, El Salvador, Colombia. He said he was in charge of troops from California, Tucson, New Jersey, San Antonio, Puerto Rico and other places. He said he wasn't supposed to write her this, but he was so proud of what his guys were doing that he couldn't keep it bottled up.

Mercedes had seen a lot of the men in her family go off to different wars. Their pictures were propped up on top of the television set in the living room. I was just relieved that I was married, had two kids and was beyond draft age.

Every day there was news about the fighting in Central America. It was as if a big pit bull was toying with this runty little Chihuahua, waiting for the moment to really clamp down and finish it off. In my mind I could see Sergeant Eddie, weapons and gear hanging all over him, itching to protect the helpless, find the bullies and blow them away.

I think Eddie believed all that noise about revolution was just a smoke screen for a few guys to take power. It was king-of-the-mountain all over again, just like when we played war up in the hills or at the river. Good guys, bad guys, and whoever won called themselves the good guys. If you lost, you went back at it again the next day. But Eddie knew better. He never played war with us because he knew he'd never lose, he'd never have a next day.

I think he believed that people against the war were just being taken in. They weren't born fighters like him. They were just people like me and my wife, people who needed protection. So when American troops began to die, I was glad Godzilla was down there kicking butt.

≈  ⌒

I'm an accountant for the county. I like to see the world through numbers— easier to understand that way. Maybe that's a weakness because I'm always trying to reduce everything to figures, though a lot of times I can't. "Math doesn't lie," my favorite teacher Mrs. Cooper used to say. If you were smart enough and had all the numbers, you could figure out anything. Debts, credits, population, GNP—everything would fit into a balance sheet. She'd work out an equation showing how in X place, trouble would break out in a certain year.

At first, I liked the formulas but I couldn't relate the numbers to actual people, people like my grandmother or me and my family. I couldn't connect us or Eddie to figures on a chalkboard.

One day in mid-summer I came home, depressed by smog, heat and traffic, thinking I just wanted to sit by the fan and not talk to anyone. A cold beer and a thoughtless, numberless mind is all I wanted. But when I got to the house and walked in the front door, there was my wife in front of the television shrieking.

"Look, it's Eddie! Eddie!"

And there he was, filling up the screen being interviewed by some lady with a microphone. He looked tired and grimy but his eyes were alert. He kept looking away from the camera, nodding or saying something quick to somebody you couldn't see. Then he'd turn back to the interviewer to answer her questions.

"We're here and we'll stay here," he was saying.

"Sergeant Vera," the woman said, "your commanding officer has ordered you and your men to release the president, yet you refuse . . . "

Just then the screen turned fuzzy gray, then black, and we waited. After two or three minutes, the news anchor appeared and apologized for the interruption. He promised further news of the commando raid later in the broadcast or later on the 7 o'clock news. My wife said Eddie and his men had overrun the presidential palace. This was earlier in the day. Now, Eddie's commander apparently had accused him of insubordination. Eddie was in a fix. But I had to laugh.

"Why are you laughing?" my wife said. "They could shoot him for that."

"They won't shoot him."

"That's probably what happened, that's why they went off the air. You think the Army's going to let him get away with that stuff?"

Just then my son came in the front door with his friend from down the block. Both of them had sticks and were pretending to be soldiers, still shooting at the bad guys behind them in the street. My wife took away the sticks and scolded them.

"What did I say? No guns!"

"Mom, they're just sticks."

"You know what I mean."

"All right, guys," I said, switching channels and hoping for more news about Eddie. "Go play something else."

"What is it with you boys and men?" my wife said. "You guys got to have guns, got to hurt people."

"Hey, this is Eddie," I said, "not *you guys!* It's Eddie. He finally did it."

"What, get himself killed?"

"There's no way. I know Eddie and he just climbed a mountain."

My wife shook her head and walked into the kitchen. The boys had gone out the front door and I could hear them making shooting noises around the side of the house.

I thought about Eddie and his commandos. The guy who saved me in seventh grade was some kind of hero. It didn't matter that later they'd say he was deranged or had a criminal record the Army somehow missed.

So when the 7 o'clock news came on, all they could do was give opinions. They showed the presidential palace from across the street. Over the high wall you could just make out the top floor of the mansion. An officer told reporters that hostages were being held and the situation was "unclear."

In the end, what Eddie did surprised everyone, even me.

As I saw it, he had gone down there and in three months got right into the middle of things. As a commando leader he excelled and finally was put in charge of the group that first dropped from the chopper onto the palace grounds. They blasted their way into the main structure, fighting the militants who were holding the president hostage. Quick and brutal but it worked—they got their prize.

"He escaped," I said.

My wife Jackie laughed and pointed out that they were all killed. "I mean," she said, "you saw the whole building go up, right there on the screen. The president got out but no one else did."

I didn't answer her, thinking about Eddie, knowing he must have figured something out, found a tunnel, some secret exit.

"They never found his body," I said.

"But the bomb destroyed everything."

"Whatever," I said, certain Eddie and maybe some of his men had given the world the slip—before the rebels could blow up the building.

Months later, long after a new president took office, I started hearing about Eddie being talked about as some kind of Che Guevara. But they got him all wrong—he was no Che. For one thing, he wasn't political, wasn't right or left, wasn't even a good Republican. Just a fighter, a Frog Town *loco* from LA. The president might have been a bully but so were the thugs who captured him. They blew up the palace, killed a lot of people, innocent people . . . secretaries, janitors, cooks.

The other day when my son asked me about Eddie, I patted my chest.

"You mean he died?"

"No," I said, "I mean he had heart."

"But he died," my wife said.

"I didn't say that."

"I know he was your friend and all, but he died."

"You don't know that. I think he got out of there."

"If he didn't die, where is he?"

Our son looked at his mother and smiled.

About a year later, I dropped by to check on my grandmother. She said Mercedes told her a secret no one else knew. But she had to tell someone just to get it off her chest. She'd received an envelope in the mail with a picture of Eddie in it. No note, just a picture. He was standing in what looked like an Indian ruin in jeans and a T-shirt; he was smiling. My grandmother said she examined the envelope. It had no return address and was postmarked from Mérida, Yucatán.

Before leaving her house, as usual she gave me a quick blessing and made a tiny sign of the cross with her thumb on my forehead.

"*Cuídate*," she said. Then she added in carefully pronounced English, "You take care."

As I pushed open the front screen door, I raised a finger over my head. "Always do," I said, picturing Number One, at ease in a hammock by the sea, feeling a warm breeze, maybe a cool drink just within reach.

# Bedbugs

It had rained for three days and Graciela sensed she would never leave. Even if she did, the brown, muggy town would follow her home.

She lay on the thin, lumpy mattress and listened to the mad dog howl above the sound of rain hitting the metal roof. Earlier she had watched the animal chase itself, snapping at its own shadow. Someone in a plastic poncho finally collared the dog with a rope and hung the twisting, rabid body on a pole jammed into an adobe crevice.

Before the storm, Gabriela had fallen off the bed, pursued by what she thought were fleas. She complained to the hotel owner and right away he offered to share his own bed with her.

She detested the man. Not his intentions but the thick, slug like fingers, the grime around the nails, the sails of sweat running from his armpits to his waist. And there was the coarse tone of his voice.

"It's this, isn't it?" he said, pointing to the pink wriggle of a harelip scar.

"Yes," she said, hoping for an exit.

"Come here, I'm not that bad."

Gabriela shrank from the hand on the counter, almost laughing from fear. "Just do something about the fleas. If you don't, I'll move to another hotel."

"They're all the same . . . and the men will all ask you to sleep with them."

"Then I'll sleep with the fleas."

Gabriela moved stiffly toward the stairway door leading down to the street. "I'll be gone for a while," she said without turning. "And I really would love it if you did something about the fleas."

"Bedbugs, not fleas," he corrected. "They're everywhere."

"So kill them." She opened the door, then closed it behind her.

"All right!" he shouted. "But I'm telling you it never works. You can't get rid of them."

Gabriela picked a direction and stepped quickly along the high, sidewalk curb. She swung her bare arms easily, palms out. Her hands were large, feet slightly toed in, yet she carried herself with a tall gracefulness, a certain pride to her neck, her breasts and the curve in the small of her back. Even when tired, she never slouched.

As she crossed over the cobblestones in front of the small church, the man's offer echoed in her mind. A filthy man, but most likely he told the truth: it would be the same at the town's other two hotels.

Gabriela hurried into the shade of the station house and approached the clerk's window. "I'd like a ticket for tomorrow's train, please."

The large woman behind the counter looked up. "What was that?"

"Tomorrow morning's train to Sal . . . "

"Speak up, I don't hear too well." The woman peered at Gabriela above the rims of her reading glasses.

"I said I'd like to buy a ticket for tomorrow's train."

"Can't you read? The sign says trains run Monday and Thursday. Today's Tuesday. Come back tomorrow and I'll sell you a ticket." The woman daintily shifted her bulk, blew her nose into a tissue and then straightened her blouse with a tug. "I'm only here to take in the mail," she added, apologizing for her congestion and pointing outside to the small signs, one for the post office and the other for the train tickets.

Gabriela stared at the pinched, sour face for a moment. The woman began to file a fingernail. More than the humidity and heat, Gabriela concluded, the isolation here must produce that languid, witless expression in the woman's eyes, a droop in her lips.

"I said come back tomorrow."

"Then could you tell me if there's a bus that comes through here?"

"Maybe."

"How's that?"

"It depends. Maybe a flat tire, maybe an accident, maybe it rains . . . maybe the driver doesn't feel like working."

Gabriela watched the shiny metal file scratch back and forth. On the counter, a thick roll of tickets propped up an open comic book filled with colorful illustrations depicting what looked like romance stories.

"Do you know where the buses leave from . . . that is, when they are no accidents and the drivers want to drive?"

"You think I'm stupid."

"What?"

"That I don't know things."

"I didn't say that."

"Well, you're right. I got an empty head."

Gabriela's eyes opened wide.

"I do. It's because of this place. People come here for one reason and then they leave. No one wants to stay. They go look at the ruins and the famous cave and then they leave as fast as they can. Like there's a disease and they don't want to breathe the air."

Gabriela listened politely, nodding as the woman made a stinky-smell face.

"Why don't you stay a few days? Don't be like everyone else."

"Really, I've got to leave."

"Tell me what's happening outside. I mean outside this place."

Gabriela stepped back. "What about the bus?"

The woman stabbed the nail file into the counter top. "Tomorrow morning about ten. It leaves from here."

"Thanks."

Gabriela had already visited the ruins, had walked the mile along the creek bank to see the fallen stones, bought a cold soda from a grizzled vendor who stood by the "sacred" spring and listened to the sales pitch of a local shirtless boy who promised to lead her beyond the burial caves. It was there, he said, that the first human inhabitants of the New World discovered the miraculous tunnel to "the other side."

Gabriela finished swallowing the overly sweetened soda. "What's on the other side?"

"A paradise," the boy said.

"No."

"Yes!"

"How come there's nothing in the guide book about a tunnel?"

"It's a secret."

"Just show me the caves."

"You'll be sorry."

"The caves, let's go."

Gabriela followed the boy along the bottom of a chalky granite cliff. There were no other visitors; she had seen no other tourist in town. "How far to the caves?"

"Pretty soon," the boy said and skipped ahead on the dirt path.

That's when Gabriela, suddenly feeling an odd hyper-awareness, stopped and said she was going back to the ruins. She spun around and hurried along, sensing the boy and who-knows-who-else trailing her. She heard him calling for her to stop and wait for him. But now she was running. By the time she reached the spring where the water bubbled out from among the blocks of stone, she realized she was alone—the old man selling sodas was gone. She heard footsteps behind, whirled around and faced her young guide.

"I have to go," he said, his eyes darting beyond her and to the sides. "You'll give me something?" he said, extending an open hand.

"For what?"

"I brought you here. You almost saw paradise."

"Fine," Gabriela said, smiling as she pinched up paper currency from the pocket of her jeans, gave it to him then watched the slender figure disappear into the brush.

Later, when Gabriela was about to leave the train station counter, she was warned about the bus drivers. "They all drink a lot," the big, congested clerk said. "Stick with trains. They stay on the tracks."

"Right."

"You want to stay on the tracks. On the tracks, sweetie, on the tracks I always say."

Gabriela left the repetitive, phlegmy ticket seller without a glance back. Even in the street under the heavy gray sky, she felt a tightness in the air, a narrowing of spaces, the certainty of tropical plants growing too fast. How could she escape the suffocation of all the incessant greenness, of vines and leaves and weeds, of cobblestone and dry, crusted streets, of thick white walls, of the curious, blank stares of strangers under the shade of wrinkled hands?

"Postcards!" a short man in a patchy shirt and trousers shouted. "Buy some postcards—or just one!"

He approached the sweaty stranger and with one hand, in a lazy flourish, he made a rainbow fan of the postcards, all of the same scene: the ancient structure of stones with the spring of water pooling in the center toward the bottom.

"Pick a postcard, young lady."

The vendor's hair sprouted at the top of his head in dirt-colored tufts. One eye peered off to the side and his blotchy, wet forehead came close, almost touching her arm. He grinned and displayed a grotesque line of stained teeth. Gabriela remained still. The man gave out a sudden, hollow laugh, then walked away counting each postcard as if counting his fingers.

Gabriela stopped under a dying oak tree that tilted over one corner of the plaza. Above the huge, scarred trunk a few patches of leaves drooped motionless from the only live branches. Leaning against the tree, she scanned the plaza, waiting for movement on the streets or in the shadows. Occasionally figures moved across the plaza or along the fronts of the low buildings. A noisy, dusty car bounced by, followed a while later by an even noisier, dustier pickup truck.

"Why go?" Roberto had asked her at home. "Why go *there?*"

"I don't know, why stay here?" she had answered, then added, "I have to get away. I can't take it anymore."

Her boyfriend had placed a hand on her forearm. "Move out, get an apartment somewhere."

"No, I've got to go away."

"Stay with me. I'll make room."

"What for? So I can call her every day, listen to the same thing? She doesn't talk to anybody else—not him, not my brothers, nobody but me. How sick is that?"

Gabriela had walked to the window where she could see the patio. She hated to explain, especially to Roberto, whose patient, probing eyes were like pig snouts burrowing in the garbage. Eventually he would discover something and she didn't want to explain, didn't want to say she was tired of watching her mother plunge a knife into the silence of a man she had loved until he changed into a stranger.

"No, no questions now, Roberto. I don't want your hands and your patience or your bed . . . maybe later but not now. I don't know what it is but not now."

"Why?" he had asked again.

Gabriela had wiped her moist hands on her hips, pressing hard on the cotton dress as if she were squeezing blood into her loins. "Not now!" she had told him. "I can't tell you but I have to leave."

"What about your job?"

"They'll get a substitute teacher."

Gabriela had expected a smile. "Say something easy, Roberto. Make it seem perfectly normal for a young woman to escape into nowhere. Explain it to me, since maybe you think you know. Tell me about this silly, freed bird that refuses to rest even when she sleeps."

Roberto had been silent; he did smile but only for an instant, perhaps a hurt smile. Gabriela couldn't tell because at that moment she saw her father's car swing into the driveway.

On cue Roberto had given her a quick kiss on the cheek, waved goodbye and left by the back door.

≈  ≈

The rabid dog spun into the plaza, followed by a group of screaming, raggedy kids. With sticks and rocks they chased him toward the big tree in the plaza. The closer the dog came, the harder Gabriela pressed her back against the rough surface of the tree trunk. When it seemed the dog would not turn and would either smash into her legs or leap onto her chest, it swerved and the boys careened around the tree and continued the chase.

The rest of the afternoon, Gabriela sat on her bed in the hotel, sipping from a bottle of cheap rum she had purchased on her way back from the ruins. With her notebook on her knees she was trying to state her impressions of the trip so far. She had purposely omitted bringing books to read. "I want to turn myself inside-out," she had told her mother. "Where I'm going I don't want to think because there's too much to see, to do."

Gabriela struggled with the simplest words, afraid to describe what she had found. The place of the ruins was all she could manage, but there were no people. And the path to paradise had to have been something else in a boy's scheme or dream.

At night the rain began, softly at first, then with the weight of a cloudburst. In the morning—although the daylight barely cast a shadow in the room—the rain continued. For three days the water came down.

Gabriela ate her meals in silence with the other guests. A light bulb dangled from a taped cord above the long, food-stained table. At dinner during the first night of the rain, the hotel owner, in his typically crude manner, announced that the four guests should eat very slowly and make the meal last as long as possible, ". . . since there's nothing else to do."

The two Spaniards, older men with grim expressions, ignored the comment. But Gabriela and the nervous shoe salesman turned to watch the thick-bodied man swagger into the soot-blackened kitchen, "to encourage the cook in her labors." When it rained this hard, he had warned, the train never came and the buses and trucks almost never passed the first mudslide. The Spaniards grumbled and went off to play checkers over drinks, and the shoe salesman politely excused himself, saying he wanted to read his Bible.

On the second day of the rain, Gabriela wrote five pages of scenery descriptions in a jerky scrawl. The words seemed cramped with odors and sounds, the taste of fruit and the movement of flesh. Toward the end of this entry, the hotel owner crept onto the fifth page, and though she tried to keep him from her thoughts, slowly she filled the last paragraph with his sweat and dirt and rough, ugly pleas for a few minutes to lie beside her. Beer-bloated and with clumsy fingers, he chipped away at her shell like an amateur who knows the pearl is inside but chooses to bash away until it's there, in the palm of his hand.

By the afternoon of the third day, Gabriela stopped writing. She ripped the notebook and dropped the pages into the metal washbasin, followed by a lit match. Now there was only fire, the sound of rain on the metal roof, as well as the image of the mad dog, twitching, finally silent.

Gabriela snapped the bed sheets free of the bedbugs, beat the mattress surface, and then neatly tucked in the two sheets. After removing her clothes, she stretched herself out on the bed—legs together, hands by her thighs—and waited.

For a long while she waited. Then they came. One by one, two or three at a time, she didn't know. But they came. She could feel them. And still she waited, letting them bite, waiting, watching the room turn dark with the coming of night.

# Awakening

Despite three cups of strong coffee, Martin Medina began to nod off. When his chin thumped down on his chest, he jerked back and blinked himself awake. The speaker had just finished, so Medina joined the clapping. Soon he began to drift again. A Los Angeles book dealer, he was in London at a conference of antiquarians, feeling powerless against the effects of jet lag and the comfort of a cushioned seat in the middle of the sixth row.

As soon as the next speaker was introduced, he began to squirm, tightening and relaxing his buttocks, a sleep-fighting trick he'd learned in grammar school. But all his pinching and squeezing did not work. The voice droned on about damage to paper and parchment and how to combat acid damage, which Medina heard as *sasid samidge*. And the word *map* sounded seductively like *nap*.

"Excuse me," his neighbor to the right whispered.

Medina turned to face the pointy pink nose of a white-haired woman. Thinking he might have snorted or snored, he apologized.

"Nonsense," the woman said, handing him the folded newspaper that had slipped from his knees. "Wish I could escape as easily. The chap's a bit of a bore."

Medina smiled and glanced down at the *Telegraph* classifieds on his lap. His wife Sandra had gone off to tour museums, and he was supposed to meet her for dinner at the hotel by seven. So it was a matter of staying awake until then.

Near-sighted, he removed his wire-rimmed glasses and began skimming the notices. He was hoping for anything interesting—a funny word, an odd typeface, anything to kill the speaker's monotone delivery. Toward the bottom of the page he spotted a three-line announcement of a 10 a.m. estate sale in Greenwich. Squinting, he reread the tiny print, dwelling on the words *collection of old and rare books.* Suddenly alert, he leaned toward the pointy nose and announced, "Gotta go!"

The woman nodded sharply and whispered, "Yes-yes, by all means."

Clutching the newspaper in one hand, Medina stood. "Sorry."

"No need to explain," the woman said. "Nature calls."

Medina thought of explaining but stepped in front of her and moved on, careful not to step on toes or bump knees. When he reached the aisle, he pivoted and bolted for the exit.

A while later, he emerged from the North Greenwich tube station into the warm air of late spring and waved down an empty taxi. After getting in, he offered up a scrap of the newspaper page with the estate-sale circled.

The driver, a young woman with wild red hair, took the notice and read it. "Right," she said and gave it back.

"How long will it take to get there?"

"Depends."

"Excuse me?"

"On if you let me read your 'aid."

"What?"

"Your 'aid," she said and handed him a wrinkled business card.

Medina took the card, pushed his bifocals snugly onto the bridge of his nose and read the words in the center: *Mary Clear, Phrenologist.* A Dagenham address and telephone number rippled across the bottom.

He stared at the name and title. He'd never met a phrenologist.

"I read 'aids," the woman explained. "'Finology?'"

"Yes, I know," Medina answered, returning the card.

"Well?"

Medina glanced at his watch, which showed twelve minutes to noon. "I just want to go to this address."

"Suit yourself."

"How long will it take to get there?"

"Not long."

He slid back on the seat and closed his eyes as the cab accelerated, braked, turned, accelerated, slowed, bumping along. He and Mary Clear were both quiet, the street noise of engines and tires on the pavement coming strongest from her open window. He sat up and looked at the billow of Orphan Annie curls now partially blocking his view of the road ahead. He was about to ask how much longer it would take to reach the address he'd shown her when the cab swerved to the left, slowed and stopped at the curb.

"Well?" she said.

"Well what?"

"Your 'aid?"

"We there?"

"Almost but I 'afta read it first."

"I don't think . . . "

"Please."

"No."

"Only take a minute."

Mary Clear shifted her body around and looked at Medina. "Sir! A few minutes—for practice."

"Practice?"

"I'm in training."

Medina removed his glasses and bent forward to retrieve the piece of newspaper that had fallen by his feet. He intended to read the address for her but then he felt her fingers on the crown of his head. Instantly, a pleasurable wave descended through his body; thoughts faded to sensations.

"All right," she said with a perky, Cockney lilt, "so whot we 'av 'ere?"

Medina listened to her describe his traits. As her fingertips moved over his nearly naked dome, he wondered "what harm could she do? All hokum anyway, a kind of cranial palm reading. She's a student in training. Let the girl train, practice all she wants."

Her hands moved off the top of his head and onto the furrows above his eyebrows, then around to the thinning, gray sides of his temples. He heard in her cheerful voice the words "spontaneous . . . curious . . . vigorous." The pleasing patter continued as her fingers inch-wormed their way over his head, pausing now and then before moving on.

Head tilted forward, eyes closed, Medina dreamily wondered how he must look to anyone walking by. He pictured the frizzy-haired figure kneeling on the front seat, her rump facing the dashboard, arms extended, hands busy.

Her voice now turned soothing. The last word he heard before dozing off was, "lucky."

Medina's motionless forehead was resting on the top of the seat when he heard an insistent, "Wake up, sir! Wake up!"

Mary Clear tugged at one ear. Medina raised his head. His eyes began to adjust to the sudden light, and then the young face, all freckles and concern, came into focus.

"Your features are balanced, even keeled," she announced.

Medina smiled, thinking Sandra should hear this. After almost half a lifetime with her, he knew his wife would never say his ship was steady, especially since his business had started to list badly—actually, to fail and head to the bottom.

In the past several years his bookstore had barely turned a profit, losing out first to the chain stores, then to online sales and beyond that, to the entire onslaught of the electronic world. His response was paralysis and emotional benders in which he would read trancelike for days on end. He was no longer interested in selling books or talking the trade with his two employees. In dealing with customers, some of them long-time regulars, he could no longer muster enthusiasm for bookish chitchat.

Medina moped, ignoring his usual morning jog in Griffith Park. His son, a lawyer in the district attorney's office, tried and failed to argue him out of his funk. Movies, dinners out, visits with the grandkids, an overnighter to Catalina Island—whatever he and Sandra did, Medina's mood remained gloomy. His son urged him to write fiction again, making it sound as simple as opening a door, which in a way had been bolted and nailed shut for years. As a young man he had published three short stories and wrote two unpublished novels of adventures he never had. Medina scoffed at his son's suggestion, saying his imagination had wandered off a long time ago. Now, he preferred to sit and read.

So Sandra proposed a trip to London. Maybe the conference would ignite some fires.

"That's it, sir."

"Huh?"

"We're 'ere . . . your address."

Medina peered through the side window at a two-story brick building set back from the street behind a low, stone wall.

"Wouldda told you before but I wanted me practice."

"It's okay," Medina said, running a hand over his scalp. He stepped out onto the sidewalk and was about to ask her what the fare was, since he hadn't seen a meter, when the cab pulled away. Puzzled, he watched the boxy black shape turn the corner and disappear.

"Well, thanks for the rub," he whispered to himself.

He crossed the sidewalk and stepped onto the U-shaped driveway. An assortment of cars, trucks and vans were parked on the grass on both sides of the asphalt all the way around the U to the exit side. Here and there men and women carried boxes, framed paintings, lamps, chairs, bundles of clothes and what looked like drapes.

At the front entrance, Medina waited behind a line of visitors filing past a white-haired man in faded jeans. Medina expected to see a brochure or at least a list of sale items tacked up somewhere.

"Welcome, ladies, gents," the man said. "Everything's marked. The clerk in the kitchen will be happy to take your money."

Medina stepped into the crowded foyer. "Unless there's nothing of value inside, why no auction, why no professionals? Seems more like a garage sale," Medina thought.

"How about books?" he called back.

"In the library!" the greeter at the door shouted. "And the attic!"

Medina moved along with the current of bodies, first to the right, then to the left. He let himself be carried into the high-ceilinged dining room, through a long living room and finally into an eddy of people in the wood-paneled library. He glanced around, decided where to start and went to work.

In less than twenty minutes he had checked all the shelves without finding a book he might buy. A conventional collection, it included English standards from Shakespeare to Thackeray, novels, histories, some science, some untranslated Russian and French authors, volumes of Twain and several encyclopedia sets. There were also plenty of works by forgotten country preachers and moralists telling readers of the seventeenth and eighteenth centuries how to live.

Whoever died and left the estate obviously wasn't too concerned about appearance or value. On one wall alone, rows of paperback potboilers were mixed in with a number of first-edition Huxleys and Greenes, an early *Ulysses*, an abridged *Don Quixote* in English, even a good-condition, first edition of *Under the Volcano*, unsigned.

Most of the people Medina saw around him seemed to be searching for bargains, not books. They resembled hunting dogs glancing about in quick, jerky motions until they spotted something and sprang forward. A Tiffany lampshade, a pair of brass sconces, a reading chair with claw feet, an end-table, ivory figurines of bearded men, oil paintings depicting sailing ships at sea, stone bookends, brocaded drapery and curtain rods. Amid the helter-skelter of grabbing, only a few people were holding books.

Medina left the room and followed the paper sign that pointed the way up two flights of stairs to the attic. Reaching the topmost landing, he entered a long, dimly lit room with sloped ceilings. In one corner, hidden behind several wicker chairs and a dismantled, four-poster bed, he found a wall of sagging shelves loaded with books and stacks of magazines. He brushed away cobwebs.

Under the light of a dangling, overhead bulb, he squinted to read the titles, now and then pulling something out, blowing off the dust and looking inside the cover. He did this methodically, moving along each shelf from left to right.

In earlier years, when he checked a collection he would concern himself with the tastes of his serious clients, trying to match their interests and requests with purchases made at trade fairs and auctions or through online searches and the booksellers' grapevine. But with business sagging, his attention to customers had waned; he no longer hunted for treasures to buy and sell. Another impulse seemed to be urging him out of his gloom. Every day at home or at the store he would sit before the computer searching sites, reading articles and even entire books on the screen. He would read until someone roused him.

Medina told Sandra it wasn't an addiction so much as a mental itch he couldn't scratch because it wasn't physical. Several years ago while both were in bed, he tried to explain it to her another way: "It's like a yearning or craving, not constant but when it's there, I get this thing . . . this . . . this need to know things, get answers . . . for . . . for . . . "

"For?"

"Clarity."

"For clarity."

"Yes. I want to see it all."

"All what?"

"You know, how it all happened."

"Sweetie, I'm not following you."

"*Us!* You, me, everybody."

"Everybody?"

"Me, then. Why am I here?"

Sandra raised an eyebrow.

"Think about it," Medina said. "Over the centuries millions of humans have lived and died so you and I could be here. We're the result of everything that's ever happened. There's a reason why we're here and others aren't."

"So?"

"Fate."

"Correct."

"Luck."

"Uh-huh."

"Why are we who we are? Why are *you* you? Why am *I* me?"

"Not following you. Can this wait?"

"Why are we short, tall, smart, dumb, healthy, sickly, different skin color, different hair, different features?"

"Genes, evolution, how do I know?"

"How did we get where we are?"

"Go to sleep, Marty."

"Individually, I mean."

Sandra smacked her pillow with her right hand to puff it up on one side, then plopped her head down.

"Take our ancestors," Medina said, eyes fixed on the ceiling glow from a night light in a wall socket.

"Marty, can this wait till tomorrow?"

"My ancestors in Mexico, the whole mixture—Indians, Spaniards, Africans, Chinese, even English . . . "

"I'm sleepy."

"Who were they?"

"Sweetie."

"They had full lives—work, kids, dreams, names, *thoughts!*"

"Marty."

"*Thoughts!* What were they?"

"Marty."

"Imagine . . . "

"Martin!"

"What?"

"Go to sleep."

"Right."

"Sleep."

"Yeah . . . right."

And Sandra, barely audible: "Good."

Medina never got more specific about his itch. He felt the remedy would come to him like a message, like the sudden presence of someone or something long dead or destroyed but still alive. It would come to him if he only kept searching.

At the estate sale in Greenwich, he was on his creaky left knee when his hand reached for a dark brown folder in the middle of the bottom shelf. It wasn't so much a folder as a collection of pages kept together between leather covers so stiff and cracked that they resembled brittle sheets of dry, thin wood.

He rose and moved to where the light was better and studied the crude, disintegrating threads of the binding as well as a name that had been jaggedly tooled into the surface. The name was Joseph Fields.

When he tried to lift the top cover with his left hand, it came off completely. Only his right hand and arm held the rest of the pages. Medina stared down, then felt the fragile paper with his thumb and forefinger, judging it was made of a rag material. He focused on the lopsided letters at the top of the page, the ink uneven, dark in some spots, light in others:

*I Joseph Fields lived one and twenty yeeres as prisoner, slave, servaynt and seaman in Newe Spaine—I tell my storie as a true*

*record of such life—I am an orphan whose parents and sister died
in the plague in Greenwich which I left for London where I was
taken into Christ's Hospital to live and continyud to reade and
wryte as my father a scrivener taught me and at twelve yeeres I
went to seeke worke at laste finding such in Chatham on Her
Majesty's ship Mynion where she was ankered and later in October
1567 where she departed the port of Plymouth in the Fleete of our
generall Master John Hawkyns destyned for Africa and the Indies*

Medina glanced up, staring blankly through the musty,
dusty attic. A delicious anxiety arose from his stomach and
chest. He moved to one of the wicker chairs, wiped off the seat
with a handkerchief, sat down and began to read, slowly, growing used to the bumpy writing but accustomed to the old syn-
tax and quirky spellings.

Hours later, he finished reading the fragile manuscript. For
a long while he sat in a daze, knowing he had finally scratched
the itch. The journal story of Joseph Fields gave Medina a
shove toward the clarity he thought he might never have.
Closing his eyes, he saw, heard and felt things from another
time as alive and fresh as if *he* were the ship's boy cast ashore
with other starving shipmates.

*I kept telling myself to move and keep a fix on the others and on
the trees and not on the black muck holding and sucking at my feet
and me thinking please God if only I can reach the beach and sand
there by the trees where the others are stretched in the shade*

"Hello?" a man's voice called into the attic. "We're closing."

Medina opened his eyes and shouted, "Yes! Coming!"

He stood up, the manuscript held to his chest, and hurried to the doorway. At the top of the stairs, he breathed deeply and slowly descended.

Downstairs he found that most of the prospective buyers and the estate's objects were gone. In the big living room, two women were collapsing foldup chairs and several men were fussing over whatever was in a large box. Medina headed to the kitchen, where an unusually thin, bespectacled man sat at a long wooden table with a receipt pad, metal box, pens and a machine for swiping credit cards. He was listening to a small radio, rooting for his team.

"What did you find?" the man asked in a voice that rattled in a gargling way, as if he'd had an operation on his vocal cords.

"Some old papers," Medina said with a dismissive air.

"That so?" the man said, lowering the excited voice shrieking from the radio speaker.

Medina shrugged, and the sides of his mouth tilted downward.

The cashier extended a hand. "Let's have a look."

Medina hesitated, then set the manuscript on the table, remarking that it was falling apart, that it might be too much trouble to have it properly bound.

"I see that," the man said.

Medina wiped his face with a handkerchief. "Seems to be some sort of personal journal."

Just then a young couple entered the kitchen, the man holding two table lamps, the woman toting a child snugly on her hip.

The skeletal man rubbed his forehead. "Well," he said, "I don't know. What do you think it's worth?"

Guessing the man was an antiquarian rube, Medina blurted, "Five pounds!"

The seller shook his head. "I don't think so."

Medina waited while the seller pondered the matter. "Must be at least seven."

"Six then," Medina said.

"Fine," the man replied, stretching a spectral arm to the radio and turning up the volume with his bony fingers. The young man stepped closer, lampshades raised like elephant ears.

Medina opened his wallet, plucked out the bills and set them on the table.

The old man coughed, stopped the rattle in his throat and then put the bills in the metal box. "Not my real job, you know," he said. "Actually, I'm in security."

Medina turned slightly and looked back as if his heist were about to be discovered. The man with the lamp ears focused on the radio.

"My cousin's the book nut," the seller continued. "He's sick and I cover for him." The man handed Medina a paper bag from a stack of bags behind him on the counter. "Here you go," he said. "Put the lot in here."

Medina carefully slipped his prize into the bag, said thank you and edged past the young couple practically on tiptoes. He hadn't felt such a thrill over a purchase since he was ten and forked over his entire paper-route savings for an early edition of *Treasure Island.*

By the time he emerged into dusky light from the Hyde Park tube station, he was desperate to relieve himself. Still hugging the bag with the manuscript, he jogged on the sidewalk to a street corner with a public restroom sign. In minutes he stood at a urinal, blissful and oblivious. When he finished he tried zipping up his trousers with one hand while gripping the bag with the other hand. Then he heard footsteps. He started to turn around and then everything stopped.

The next morning he woke up in a brightly lit hospital room. Woozy, he looked up and slowly focused on Sandra's face staring at him.

"Welcome back."

"Wha . . . ?"

"Clunked on the head . . . robbed."

Medina nodded and slowly gazed around the room. Sunlight filtered through partially closed blinds, a blank television screen hung from a wall. On the right side of his bed, wires attached to his chest led to a blipping heart monitor and screen.

Sandra said a jogger found him unconscious on the restroom floor.

Medina tried to sit up, and she gently pushed him back. "Easy—you have a concussion," Sandra said, adjusting the pillows behind his bandaged head. "They found your wallet in the bushes. No money, no credit cards."

"What about a bag? Did they find a bag?"

"No, no bag."

"A paper bag."

"Nothing about a bag."

Medina's eyes glistened and his breathing turned short and shallow.

In moments, a nurse entered the room and glanced at the monitor. "Have a problem, do we?"

"Marty," Sandra said, "calm down. I cancelled the cards. Nobody had used them."

The nurse leaned over the bed and placed his hands in hers. "Mister Medina, you have to relax. Your heart's racing."

Medina looked at the ceiling, one tear dropping onto the sheet.

"Try closing your eyes," the nurse said. "Think of a pretty place, somewhere you can stretch out and relax, somewhere beautiful, peaceful, a relaxing place, the perfect place to relax. Just imagine it . . . and relax, relax."

Sandra frowned and stared at her husband, whose strained expression seemed to be softening.

"Go on," the nurse said in a soft, sweet voice. "Try. Think of the perfect place, sweet and comfortable, a paradise just for you."

Medina lowered his head onto the pillow, eyelids fluttering. The nurse repeated herself and soon the agitated patient stopped squeezing her hands. He could see the beach and then hear Joseph Fields crawling onto land: *smooth sand on my face and hands and arms and then onto this soft warm place out of the muck and water and onto the beach and then dear god moving into the shade under the trees with the others.*

Police searched trash bins and a wide area around the restroom. They questioned the usual park denizens, from bird watchers to vagrants, and followed up on several reports of empty shopping bags found in the area. And a broken cell phone thought to be Medina's was found in nearby bushes, but Medina had always been device-free, stubbornly vocal about being untethered from the digitized world.

The assault and theft briefly made the news, generating sympathetic letters and online comments, although several writers referred to the "alleged manuscript" of a middle-aged man who'd been bopped on the head.

Medina himself appeared uncertain about the specifics of the stolen item, which only fed the impression that he had invented the manuscript theft. In his first and only interview, he said, "It's not worth much and maybe it's only value is nostalgic, but all I ask is that the person who has it, please, I beg you, give it back."

A police spokesman explained that the manuscript could be returned anonymously by simply wrapping it in paper with the word *Medina* on the outside and depositing the item in a public post box. The Royal Mail would then forward it by special delivery to the Los Angeles book dealer.

Local antiquarians familiar with the eccentricities of the rare-book fringe, generally believed Medina was either delusional and invented the theft or had truly lost something of great value and didn't want to tip his hand to the thief.

Sandra kept doubts to herself, although after her husband's four-day hospital stay, she cheerfully helped him retrace his movements on the afternoon of the estate sale. But they could not find the cab-driving phrenologist, Mary Clear. The Dagenham address and telephone number on her card were bogus, and the London Taxi Driver's Association had no record of such a driver. Medina spoke to a dozen or so Greenwich cab drivers, describing a freckle-faced young woman with wild red hair. "She's a fake, mate," one driver bluntly told him. Medina avoided mentioning that she had read his head; earlier when he'd told police about this, some detectives had chuckled, inferring something else.

Medina and Sandra also cruised the streets of Greenwich in a licensed cab until he finally spotted the place where he thought the sale was held. The old structure looked empty, ghostly. A kitchen window was broken and bits of paper and junk mail were scattered over the driveway and on the dry grass.

"This is it," Medina said when they reached the entrance. He stepped around a patch of weedy rose bushes and peered into the kitchen through a dirty pane. "Right there. I bought it right there from a skinny old man who didn't have a clue what he was selling me."

"Marty, let's go."

"I was standing right there in the kitchen!"

"Come on," Sandra said, turning toward the street. She waved an arm forward as if to pull him after her. "Nothing's here."

Martin Medina never did recover the manuscript. He and Sandra returned to Los Angeles, where their son helped them sell the bookstore to a coffee shop chain that needed classics and leather-bound volumes for decoration. Medina sold the rest, keeping only a few treasures.

Then, several months later and still possessed by a relentless, stubborn memory, he sat down at his desk and placed a sheet of good-quality paper squarely before him. He removed the cap of his new, gold-plated fountain pen and wondered what Joseph Fields, the enslaved son of a scrivener, would have thought of such an instrument. For a moment Medina held the pen poised over the paper. Then with a flourish, his hand descended and he began to write.

# The Chamizal Express

I remember the bus. It was called the Chamizal Express, and it always left around dawn before anyone was awake. Rudy, the driver, must have been awake, but I never noticed because he was always so quiet.

The old bus had been dug out of the dirt and weeds, patched together again, painted and supplied with leather-covered front seats. It was named Chamizal because that's where they found it, in that wasted piece of no-man's land between Texas and Chihuahua—a place, as my aunt would say, neither here nor there, *ni de este lado ni del otro*.

One morning I climbed on with all the other half-asleep passengers, eventually found an empty seat, one by a window, and waited for the bus to move. We all waited. Then we slowly opened our eyes and began to crane our necks and wonder why there was no driver. Finally someone whistled and Rudy appeared, swung into the driver's seat, pumped the gas pedal and started the engine. I remember that some days the bus would move; other days the gears would churn into a kind of silence and Rudy would gesture for us to be patient. On those days a few of the men and women—some with children— would leave, muttering as they hurried off toward the regular bus stop further down the highway.

This time, however, the Chamizal seemed to jump forward as if it were eager to get moving. The stars still lit the sky, the air was cool, and everyone appeared to settle back for a bit more sleep before the heat and noise of the day began. I had turned in my seat, facing the window, eyes closed, when something began pushing into my back. It was my neighbor's knee. In trying to get comfortable, this person—the stranger on the seat next to me—had folded one of her legs onto the seat so that her knee projected into my spine.

I shifted slightly, thinking the movement would rouse her enough to pull her knee back. Nothing, not a muscle moved; she was lost in sleep. From the light of the half moon I could see her perfectly shaped teeth, her dark lips and a small, delicate nose, nostrils tightening, then relaxing with each deep breath. Her sleep seemed so profound, so active, you might say, that I decided not to bother her. The knee would remain where it was, and I would have to sit facing forward and as tightly as possible against the window-side of the bus.

Carefully, I moved into this position, and since I was now thoroughly awake I began to worry about not being able to sleep. I counted stars, then imagined my aunt peacefully smoking her pipe. But nothing worked, I couldn't sleep, and from the hint of blue in the sky I knew it would soon be light. "Why me," I thought. "Everyone but me has escaped."

The snoring grew louder, and from the smell of things, I'm sure some of the passengers had relaxed completely. Apparently Rudy now felt he was safe and that no one would notice, because he began to swerve and zigzag across the highway. Once he even stood up and let go of the steering wheel, laughing like a wild man, his red shirt rippling behind him in the wind coming from the open window.

That's when I first clutched at my neighbor's knee. But it was only after Rudy sat down that I realized my hand was gripping warm, smooth skin. I removed my hand and looked up to see that same, soft face of an angel.

Suddenly, the bus lurched to one side and my neighbor immediately fell on top of me. She was now lying across my lap and chest, still asleep. In fact, as I looked around in the shadows and half-light I could see that everyone was asleep, even though some of them had been thrown against each other. The next lurch went the other way, and this time not only were bodies thrown from one side to the other, but most of the overhead boxes, sacks and suitcases dropped onto the passengers below. I managed to protect my head with my arms. When the bus righted itself I was practically in the aisle, with my young companion draped across me, one arm flung over my shoulder. She was smiling.

I sat up straight and again glimpsed the bizarre figure of Rudy. This time he was steering with one foot on the wheel, his body hanging like a monkey from the overhead handrails. The Chamizal Express had left the highway and seemed to be rolling down a long, bumpy slope. That's when Rudy dropped to the floor, turned off the headlights and said the only words I've ever heard him speak: "*Hasta luego*." Then he jumped out of the bus and I heard him laugh one last time.

For a moment I thought my lovely, young seatmate was awake because she embraced me, kissed me on the lips and pressed her body against mine. I wanted to go on smelling the faint, sweet scent of her hair, wanted her to press even closer, but I knew that if I didn't stop the bus, no one would. And the Chamizal seemed to be moving faster now, pitching and bouncing as crazily as a ship in a storm. I began to feel sick, yet a sudden drowsiness had entered my head. I had to stop the bus or we would all die.

She kissed me again but this time she followed it up by asking my name. I couldn't believe it. Here we were, being thrown from side to side, about to crash into who knows what, and she asks me ever so calmly, "What's your name?"

I started to answer, thinking I should enjoy the moment, when suddenly the bus ride became smooth, level, quieter. I looked at my angel.

"What's *your* name?" I asked, holding her in my arms, happy we were both still alive.

"Linda," she whispered.

In those sweet moments just before sunrise, I looked around and could see the other passengers starting to stretch and yawn. "Where are we going?" I asked, no longer feeling sick and now wanting to sleep.

I vaguely remember the haze of early dawn. The bus rolled to a stop, a sound like footsteps on gravel came closer, and Rudy—all smiles—hopped up to the driver's seat and started the engine.

"Sleep," Linda said softly. The Chamizal shifted into fourth or fifth gear. I slumped back, and my knee flopped sideways against my neighbor's thigh.

"We're almost there," she whispered.

"Where?" I asked.

I couldn't catch her answer because all I could hear was the creaking and grinding of the old Chamizal as it traveled west with the sun.

# El Mago

Luisa's father called him the *curandero*. Sally's mother called him an unfortunate. The girls simply called him El Mago. Although he was older than the girls could imagine, there was no odor of age about him—only, it seemed, the smell of paper-thin, hairless skin. He was squat, fat and had nicotine stains on one hand. Luisa remembered he had a harsh brittle cough and she thought his chest was like an empty milk carton filled with tiny bone particles.

On this Sunday, like many others before, the two girls sat fidgeting in their blue corduroy jumpers and plain white blouses, in the pew behind the nuns, listening to words about Christ and God and the Virgin and so many saints they would never keep count, all the while watching a fly rub together what looked like its hands. Or they watched the sleepy altar boy, his shoelaces untied, or played silent games with their fingers and feet, or folded and unfolded catechism pamphlets, waiting, finally tiring and waiting some more. As usual the two had gone to Mass by themselves, leaving their parents, who usually attended a later service.

Luisa and Sally had been best friends since third grade and often told strangers they were twins, even though Luisa was smaller and darker, Sally being rounder and the fair-haired *güera*. When they first met the old man he told them he wasn't fooled, but it was good to play sisters. He said this in a friendly way, not trying to hurt.

El Mago's clients called him Don Noriega. He lived alone in a shabby-looking wooden house halfway up a steep hill overlooking the old streetcar line to Glendale. The neighborhood along the LA River knew him since two generations back when he arrived from an obscure town in northern Durango. A hypnotist, soothsayer and folk doctor, he rarely left his house, receiving payment usually in the form of food or small gifts. Around the sides of his house and in the back he grew all the herbs, spices and exotic plants he needed for his cures.

His living room, which doubled as a waiting room, was lavishly decorated with thick Moroccan rugs, plaster sphinxes, pictures and figurines from pre-Colombian cultures, soft plushy chairs and odd-shaped, marble and brass antique lamps. On one side was a water-filled glass tank containing slender, yellow-and-black striped fish from the Amazon River. On the other side were two cages of colorful birds from New Guinea and the rainforests of Panama. And adjoining this room was another that was lined and divided with filled bookcases.

Luisa and Sally first visited when they accompanied Sally's grandmother on a visit about her migraines and pains in her gall bladder, which she called her *vesícula*. Before Don Noriega attended to the business of healing, he devoted a few minutes to the girls. Speaking to them in Spanish, he overcame their shyness by giving them each a piece of hard candy. And then in a raspy voice he told them not to worry about breaking things in the house. He invited them to explore whatever attracted their curiosity. When Luisa, the more awkward of the girls, tipped over a metal stand with zodiac charts on it, Don Noriega helped her prop up the stand again. Gently and with a wink, he said all things can be repaired or left behind. They're just things. But it's the damage here, and he pointed to his heart, that cannot be fixed. Then he sat down to chat with the ailing grandmother, and the girls were left to themselves.

After standing fascinated before the tank of fish, the girls moved on to another room, which was dimly lit, cluttered with boxes and books, and saturated with a strange incense. Sally's grandmother could be heard laughing in the other room. The girls began poking around, running their fingers across dusty surfaces, looking into corners. With an innocent curiosity, they held the tiny statues of half-men and half-animals which they had taken timidly from the shelves.

It wasn't long before Sally shrieked and came running out with a terrified look on her face. "There's a dead man!" she screamed.

Puzzled, Sally's grandmother looked to Don Noriega for an explanation. He sat back in his deep chair and after an unhurried draw on his cigarette, told Sally that it was a fake mummy of a boy, not even a man. He cheerfully explained what a mummy was and why people long ago used to preserve bodies. "It was a reminder," he said, "for the dead must leave something behind to remind the living of those once known and loved."

But the old woman, with Sally trembling in her arms, was set on leaving. Don Noriega went into the other room to tell Luisa she would have to go too and that they were waiting for her. He found her standing beside a small desk tinkering with the beads on the taut wires of a small, box-like instrument. In a corner, on the other side of the room, was the opened mummy case propped up against the wall. Don Noriega told Luisa she would have to go but she could come back another day. He promised to play music for her on the little instrument.

Luisa raised her eyes. "Why do you have so many weird things?"

He looked down and Luisa could see the lines deepen at the corners of his mouth, eyes softening and friendly. "If you like these things, why do you ask?"

At the door Sally eyed Don Noriega the way she might watch an unpredictable ogre. Luisa, biting her lips in thought, waved goodbye to him from the sidewalk

When the story of the mummy was told, the girls' parents told them they could never again visit "the old *brujo* without a broom," as Luisa's mother put it.

For months afterward, Luisa was torn between wanting to see him and not wanting to disobey her parents. The girls had to pass by his street every Sunday, yet Luisa never told Sally about her private wish. Walking along the weeded-over street-car tracks, Sally would invariably poke fun at "that old *mago* and his mummies." Luisa always kept silent, not knowing what to say.

≈  ≈

One Sunday, as usual, the girls left the church eager for daylight and make-believe games on the way home. But more than that, today Luisa had made up her mind. She would visit Don Noriega. When they approached the street on which he lived she would simply say goodbye to Sally and leave. She felt that seeing him was somehow worth the risk of a spanking.

"Luisa!" Sally said, looking alarmed. "You'll get in trouble."

"No, I won't."

"What d'you want to see *him* for?"

"I just do. But don't tell."

"Aren't you scared?"

Luisa looked down at the rocks and gravel between the track ties, her mind pulsing with excitement. She moved her head, side to side. "No," she said, trying to sound casual. "He even asked me to come back."

Sally squeezed the palms of her hands together. "Luisa! I wouldn't do that."

"Go ahead and tell," Luisa said, challenging her friend. "I won't get mad." She started up the hill. "Go on, Sally. Don't wait for me."

Sally stood watching her friend climb the steep sidewalk and turn at Don Noriega's house.

The front yard was cluttered with scattered and charred boards, cans, pieces of black cloth, blackened books, metal poles, wires, chairs, bottles, jars, pots with shriveled plants and the outlines of sofas exuding tufts of cotton and matted stuffing. The door was boarded closed, as were the broken windows at the driveway side. Luisa looked like a waif standing in front of a ruined dream. She felt limp and bewildered, not yet sensing the numbness of death within the paint-peeled walls.

She stepped around the marble base of a lamp and picked her way around to the rear of the house, all the while wincing at the sharp smell of charred wood. There was no back door, only a blackened doorway. She knocked softly on the frame, calling hello into the dark interior. After a moment she heard a wheezing brittle voice.

Luisa hesitated, then stepped in. She was careful not to trip, even while bumping into strange objects at every turn, going from room to room, cautiously looking into every corner and closet. A painting fell down, a plaster statue almost tipped over. She fought to control her fear. In the front room, behind the door to the street, she saw the water-filled fish tank. The little creatures were still there floating on the surface. Luisa pursed her lips. With her forefinger she pushed one of the slivers and it slipped past the others, bumping into the side of the tank.

In the silence she heard the cough again. The floorboards creaked as she stepped through the room where the mummy was, now resting on the floor. She went into the hallway, which was pierced with soft light through holes between the skeletal roof timbers. There, in the first room to the left, sat Don Noriega. He was on the edge of a bare metal cot with no mattress. Luisa stood in the doorway unable to speak but smiling.

She moved toward the cot and sat down. She closed her eyes and felt the old man's presence. Soon she heard the delicate sounds of the music box. She opened her eyes and saw the little instrument next to her. Sunlight filtered in and the notes from the strings seemed to dance and entwine themselves around the pale white rays. For a long while she sat and listened to the music.

Then she heard a shrill voice calling her. "I have to go now," Luisa whispered. She stood and for a moment could not move. Something held her back, something weighed in her chest and throat and she began to cry. Before leaving, it seemed the blurred image before her placed the small box lightly in her open hands.

In the hallway she groped toward the back door, catching the smell of incense and spices as the hot autumn wind blew through the house.

Sally was out front, hands on hips, calling her friend's name. Luisa came from around back, stepping over the mess on the ground. She held the piece of burnt wood in her hands, two wires dangling from one side.

"Wow," Sally said, "not much left."

"Yeah," Luisa said.

"What's that?" her friend asked.

Luisa seemed surprised. "What's what?"

"That thing, what you got in your hands."

"Oh, this . . ." and she held it up for Sally to inspect. "A present."

"A what?"

"A present I picked up."

"What do you want that for?"

Luisa pulled a wire loose. "Nothing, I guess. No good now." She knelt down and set it on the ground, remembering that it was not her heart she was leaving. It was just a thing, a piece of charred wood.

"Come on," Sally whined, "the place gives me the creeps."

# Stoop Labor

Chávez hurried along the wet sidewalk. His umbrella, taut against the rain, had three dime-sized holes at the very top. Stopping at the corner, he wiped away the dribble from his forehead, removed his eyeglasses and put them in his front pants pocket. Three more blocks. He cursed the gutters, filled with running mud, and beat his free hand against his thigh. He hesitated, undecided, then jumped out into the street. Before he fell, he glimpsed the sky, gray and hateful.

He scrambled to his feet and retrieved the umbrella, which had begun to float away. He glanced around to see if anyone had seen him. On the opposite side of the street, two persons huddled in the shelter of a storefront awning. The nearsighted student could see their expressions, yet he imagined a distinct giggle. Mentally he unfurled his middle finger.

When Chávez arrived at the sorority house, the downpour had almost stopped. He paused before the concrete stairs to close the umbrella. The soggy cuffs of his trousers hung sadly over his wet shoes. Seeing the gleaming white columns, he smarted at the thought of unburdening the three-story building of its trash, the refuse of thirty-eight sorority sisters. Choking a sigh, he stepped over to the driveway and slowly walked up the slope around to the back porch. The rear door was up thirteen steps—he counted them twice a week on the days he collected the sorority's trash. On the other days he avoided the unlucky steps and worked as the house gardener, mostly mowing the grass and trimming the bushes, like the thorny oleander that threatened to engulf one of the columns out front.

Today, in passing the messy, giant oleander, he let fly with an angry wad of phlegmy saliva meant for the unruly bush. But the tail end of the spittle caught on his jacket sleeve and his wrist. He shrugged, accepting such a self-inflicted slight as some kind of cosmic punishment just for waking up today.

At the rear porch he rang the doorbell and waited. He was feeling his clothing for a dry patch on which to wipe his glasses, when the screen door opened a peek. He waited.

"It's me, Chávez," he said.

The crack in the doorway closed.

"It's me, goddammit!"

Chávez felt the scrutiny. Something moved on the floor behind the door. "All right," he said and yanked it open.

A shiny-faced figure in curlers and an oversized sweatshirt stood with her legs flexed and arms raised, poised for flight.

"Put your hands down," he ordered. "I fell in the mud."

The young woman stepped backward and fled through the kitchen door.

"Jesus," Chávez muttered, "you'd think I was a rapist."

He slipped out of his jacket and threw it against the wall where coats, ponchos and umbrellas hung from hooks. Grabbing a towel from a clothes pile next to a washing machine, he wiped his face, neck and hair. The towel reeked of soap and stale sweat. He leaned against the washer and breathed deeply, hoping to relax and calm himself. His soppy clothes stuck to his legs, chest and back. His skin was clammy and he mumbled to himself. His cigarettes were wet. Stooped and tired, he pictured himself as spindly, underfed, minuscule. Finally he took his comb and pulled back his long black hair in brief, ferocious strokes. A meek line of whiteness glistened at the hair roots above his broad, brown face. As best as he could he wiped the mud from his trousers, then stamped his feet. The polish on the puckered leather of his shoes was gone.

He removed four large plastic bags from a carton dispenser and moved toward the kitchen door. He turned the doorknob and pushed. Billows of steam rolled past his face. He stood focusing. Weapon in hand, Charlie the Filipino was walloping the potatoes into mush.

"Kill 'em, Charlie, kill 'em!"

Charlie sneered and said nothing. In the corner of the cook's eye, Chávez the Mexican was moving on tiptoes toward the stove. An evil-doer. The janitor student lifted the cover of a large fry pan and sniffed.

Charlie flung the masher into the steel sink and hopped over to the stove. "What the heel you doing, boy?" he screamed.

"Just seeing what's in the pan," Chávez replied, annoyed that the question should come up for the hundredth time.

Charlie was shaking his finger. Evidently Chávez did not know his place. He was a trash collector, a gardener. "Git your ess upstairs and pick up the tresh!"

Chávez wished he could push the fierce little face into the mashed potatoes. Instead he patted the cook's bald head and walked away, stopping to poke a tray of chicken breasts neatly arranged in rows.

"You . . . you smard ess," Charlie stammered. "You be fired."

"That would be a pleasure, Charlie. Go on, get me fired. I want to be fired."

Confused, the cook wiped his hands nervously on his apron and yelled, "Madmin! You crazy madmin!"

Dragging his plastic bags, the student stumbled into the dining room. His ears seemed to quiver and he felt as if his brain had been pierced. A tall blonde was making a small, high-pitched whistling sound as she set the silver on the table. Chávez winced. He pushed his eyeglasses onto the bridge of his nose and asked her to stop. "It grates."

The young woman whistled louder, moving from place-setting to place-setting.

"Like scratching a chalkboard," Chávez said. "Please stop."

The tall blonde continued, her lips pulled back in a tight smile revealing a neat wall of white teeth.

"Bitch," Chávez said, barely audible under his breath.

Suddenly, six feet of Bermuda shorts and swinging ponytail stomped across the dining room, blocking his way.

"Move," he said.

She whistled in his face. Chávez tried to step around but she cut him off. It was an awkward moment for him. At a six-inch disadvantage in height, he was slightly built and hardly an intimidating figure.

"Look, Miss Ponderosa Pine, that's a good act. Now please move."

She studied the puny person before her. "Is the flea angry?"

"Move."

"I don't move for fleas."

Chávez tried to step around her again.

"Where are you going, flea?"

"Move aside," Chávez said, "or do I have to . . . "

Before he could think to dodge, the blonde shoved him hard in the chest. Chávez broke his fall with his hands and lay on the floor. The chandelier glistened above and the whistling resumed. Standing up, he saw that his tormentor was now distributing porcelain dishes at place settings around the long, oval table. She carried a stack of the plates in one arm and deposited each dish with the ease of a Frisbee toss.

She glanced up. "Did the flea say something . . . ? No? I thought not."

Chávez walked to the bottom of the stairway. "You jocks are all alike," he said loudly. "No finesse."

"Oh, widdow fwee has his feewings hurt."

Chávez ignored the remark and climbed the carpeted stairs. When he reached the first landing, the housemother emerged from a doorway. A middle-aged woman with a stern expression, as soon as she saw him she shrieked, "Man on the floor!"

"It's just me, Mrs. Grovner."

"I know," she said, passing him to get to the stairs, "but you're still a male."

"Thanks."

"I notice these things."

At the top of the stairway he surveyed the long, crooked rows of wastebaskets, cardboard boxes and clumps of paper lining the hallway on both sides. Ahead, someone darted from the bathroom, her head and shoulders covered by a towel, a blur of flesh and white panties below that. As the girl ducked into her room, she knocked over one of the metal cylinders and a folded pizza box spilled onto the floor.

"Knock some more over, why don't you?" Chávez shouted.

Most of the doors were open. It was the usual rush before dinner and the Saturday night party exodus, a confusion he tried to ignore by focusing on the collection routine. He tucked three of the large plastic bags under his belt and began stuffing the fourth one with refuse. He worked his way methodically down one side of the wide hallway, dragging the bag while gathering whatever he could to empty into it. Once, he kneeled and crouched down to gather up scattered used tis-

sues and cotton balls strewn on the floor. The cloying smell of
perfumes, soaps and deodorants twice made him sneeze.

At the end of his first trip up and down the hallway, he
wrapped a long twisty around the neck of the bag and leaned
it against the wall.

On the second landing he clicked the hall lights off and on
and shouted, "Trash!" As he proceeded down the hall, moving
aside now and then as the young women stepped around him,
Chávez sneezed. Shrill voices mixed with a din of music coming, it seemed, from everywhere. He was sweating, his head
throbbed, and he was thinking he might pass out, asphyxiated
by the onslaught of soaps, perfumes, deodorants, hair sprays
and other chemical and human odors. Halfway down the hallway, feeling nauseous, he hung his head over a wastebasket
and waited for the something to come up. The fumes of an
entire floor of cosmetics attacked and he became limp.

"You okay?" a voice asked.

Panic seized him. He felt the eyes of a thousand plastic
curlers watching him.

"Chávez, you don't look too good."

"I'm okay," he said, lifting his head and flipping the wastebasket contents into the open bag. "I'm good."

He stood and rushed to the end of the hallway and back
along the other side, head down, trying to be as efficient as
possible.

Chávez struggled up the stairway to the third floor. He
breathed deeply, pulled out another bag from under his belt,
and charged ahead, scooping, stamping and enveloping all
trash and litter before him. Those in the way stood back or
quickly retreated into their rooms until the hunched-over
beast had passed.

Trash became his enemy. He attacked the paper and plastic waste with a desperate ferocity. Once, he jumped on an

empty cardboard box, ripping and pounding it flat. Then he jammed it into the black plastic bag he dragged behind. Then it was on to the next triumphs over more cartons, newspapers, wrappers, magazines, bottles and cans, which he set against the wall to retrieve later.

His back ached and his leg muscles quivered and threatened to cramp. He stopped to wipe the drip from his nose. A shout from below announced five minutes to dinner. The sorority sisters hurried about, dressing, combing, borrowing clothes, brushing hair, checking mirrors, plucking eyebrows. "Out of the way, Chávez!" someone shouted. He obliged, drained of all fight.

Normally he would have teased them. But today he was a charmless, grumbling calamity. He would not speak, would not lift his head. At the end of his third-floor run, he tied the top of the bulging bag and slumped to the floor, back against the wall. With glazed eyes he watched the girls rush by for the stairway. Chávez felt like snarling but settled for a long moan with his eyes shut.

After a while he opened his eyes and could see his face mirrored in a pair of patent-leather pumps. He raised his head. He thought her thighs were too thin, her waist too high, her breasts too large. Margie was frowning.

"What's wrong, Chávez?"

"Go away."

"What is it?"

"Leave me alone."

"What's bugging you?"

"You. You all bug me."

Margie ordered him to wait and briskly walked off down the now empty hallway. She returned with a wet paper towel, which she used to take the grime off his face. Then she felt his forehead, left again and returned with two aspirins and a glass of water.

Chávez looked up. "Miss Efficiency."

"Take these," she said, thrusting the pills into his hand. "Come on, all down."

He coughed, finally gulping the water. The aspirins, stubborn to the last, dissolved in his mouth.

She bent down and helped him to his feet. Then she kissed him on the lips. "I'm late. I'll see you after dinner."

Chávez watched her hurry to the stairs and quickly descend. After a moment, he lifted the trash bag and followed her down. His trousers, crusted with mud, cracked at the knees. At the second-floor landing, he collected another bulging bag and now began the slow descent to the next floor of residents. There he grabbed the third bag, this time dragging all three, bumping down each carpeted stair, pulling them down by their necks, risking a rip, which he knew would be disastrous.

Slowly, he pulled the last taut and shiny bag off the final stair. He embraced one bag and lifted the other two with his hands and moved forward through the house lobby into the dining room. Normally he would have exited by the front entrance but he'd chosen the shortest distance between himself and the dumpster outside, thinking to hell with the housemother's previous warnings about coming through at dinner time.

Chávez stepped into one end of the big dining room, now filled with the young diners eating, talking, seemingly unaware of his presence. He staggered to the kitchen door, followed by the din of voices, laughter and the clinking of silverware on porcelain.

Charlie and his wife, who was helping him empty the last of the mashed potatoes from a big pot to a small container, sneered at the forlorn figure moving toward the porch door.

Outside, at the top of the steps, Chávez heaved his three fat children onto the lawn below. One of the bags exploded into a rainbow of litter. He looked up at the darkening sky, sighed and descended to the mess.

On his knees amid the scattered trash, he tugged out another bag from under his belt, opened it with a snap and began to gather the refuse: tissue paper, Q-tips, cotton balls, crumpled cartons, cigarette butts, cellophane wrappers, a ripped T-shirt, used tampons wrapped in toilet paper. Instead of his latex gloves, which he'd forgotten, he wore an empty bag of corn chips on one hand and on the other a Ziploc bag he discovered was smeared with peanut butter on the inside.

After he completed this chore, he wiped his hands on the grass, then hauled the trash bags to a cinderblock storage area where he flipped them into the dumpster. Afterward, he slammed down the lid with a bang. Then he climbed up the three floors of stairs, collected the bottles and cans he'd left behind and returned outside to dump his cargo in the recyclable bin.

Work done and wearing his damp jacket, Chávez headed around to the front of the big house. At the bottom of the sloping front lawn he uttered a loud groan and sank into the wetness.

"What's the matter?" Margie asked, approaching from the front steps.

"I must be crazy," Chávez said, shaking his head.

Margie coaxed him up with both hands. "You want me around?" she said.

"No, I mean yes. I mean it has nothing to do with you."

"Did you take those aspirins?"

"Yes! You saw me. I chewed them."

"Why don't you go eat? Come on, I'll ask Charlie to give you something."

"Charlie can go fuck himself."

"That serious, huh?"

"If I told you, you wouldn't believe it."

"So tell me."

"All right. I got out of bed this morning, got dressed, drank some coffee, but before I'm really awake, somebody's knocking at the door. It's the lady who owns the house. She says I've got to move out or she'll call the police. She says I'm smoking pot. She smells it every night. It comes out of my room, she says, under the door, out my window. It's suffocating. So I show her that insect stuff I burn to keep the mosquitoes away at night. I even burn a little so she can smell it. Nothing. Did I take her for an idiot? I explained that all kinds of people smoke pot like cigarettes, people walking by on the street. Maybe that's what she was smelling. But she wouldn't listen."

"So now what?

"Wait, that's not all. I went to Michener's office to get my paper back. He tells me I don't have enough footnotes and I'll have to do it over again. You could see it really hurt him to tell me. 'Sometimes footnotes are more important than the text,' he says. So I leave his office and go over to check on my loan and they tell me my application was rejected, which means I'll have to drop out for a semester."

"Can I help?" Margie leaned forward and caressed his neck with her right hand. "I can lend you something. I'll tell my dad I need a little extra this month." Margie took his hands in hers and pulled him toward the driveway. "Everyone wondered why you were so sour today. You looked pretty dirty, too."

"I fell in the rain."

The two held hands and walked around to the backyard in silence. Slowly they counted the thirteen steps up to the screen door. Margie reached for the handle but before pulling it back she squeezed his hand and faced him. "Listen, can you come up after you eat? Mrs. Grovner's going out tonight."

Chávez looked surprised, paused, then nodded. "You sure? I probably stink."

"That's why the Gods invented showers."

"Oh, wait, I can't."

Margie opened the door. "What now?"

"I got this thing, this infection."

"What?"

"An infected sweat gland."

"So?"

"It's on my penis."

"Oh."

"I went to a doctor and I'm taking a drug that'll clear it up in a few days. He said just not to irritate it."

Margie gave him a consoling look. "We'll think of something," she said. "Maybe you can use a condom. Maybe that'll work. Come on, you better get some food in your stomach or you're going to faint from hunger."

As he followed her across the porch, Chávez fished into his back pocket and frantically searched his wallet. For the first time that day he smiled.

# Canine Cool

That evening the artist gathered his friends to eat, drink and talk about his works, which filled the big living room. Paintings and sketches of German Shepherds adorned the walls and easels or hung from wires and sticks as mobiles made of stiff tortillas emblazoned with images of canine heads. In the center of the room stood a large, painted terracotta figure, looking relaxed in khaki slacks with razor creases, white tank top and black suspenders loose on the hips. Surrounded by a group of smaller statues, the big Shepherd looked magnificent with its upright ears, attentive eyes, closed jaw and a black nose with a crackle surface that looked moist.

At first everyone praised the paintings, especially the variety of scenes: leaping high to snatch a Frisbee, behind the wheel of a low-slung, vintage car, eating at McDonald's, sleeping in a hammock, smoking in noir settings with a trench coat collar pulled up, even one pooch with a captain's cap piloting an airplane.

"Cool stuff," one friend said.

"Way cool."

"Órale, check the dude in the lowrider."

"Almost looks like . . . a bear?"

"A dog, man."

"Yeah? Maybe a wolf."

"Yo, dog, it's a dog!"

"It's art, man," another friend said. "It's whatever you think it is."

The artist entered from the kitchen with a big tray of cold, opened beer bottles and two bowls of mixed nuts. A young woman dressed in a black top and torn jeans turned away from a painting, grabbed a bottle, stepped around the little dogs and stood next to the big statue. The snout was level with her eyes.

"What's it made of?" she asked.

"Clay," the artist said.

"Everything?" she said, stroking the head.

"Everything."

"He looks so real."

"Suppose to."

Another friend, a thin, older man popping a walnut into his mouth, suggested the big figure resembled a homey of his.

"Can I touch it?"

"Sure."

The man petted the nose. "Feels cool, smooth."

"Reminds me of those Colima dogs," the woman said.

"No way. Those are little and fat. This guy's big and he's got class."

The guests drank more beer and wine and after a while ate from a pile of steamy tiny tamales, corn husks off.

A bearded man drew deeply on the stubby remainder of a joint, slowly exhaled and asked, "Why so many dogs?"

"Why not?" his neighbor said. The two shared space on a sprawling bean bag cushion. "He likes dogs."

"Well, I like the homey in the middle," said the woman who had mentioned the dancing Colima dogs. "He's a fine specimen."

"Of what?"

"I don't know, of doghood, manhood . . . easy confidence, something like that."

"Like they're all the same. I mean, like, like . . . it's all dogs."

"So?"

"Same kind of dog."

"Yeah."

"Like clones."

"Maybe that's what he's saying."

The artist and his wife didn't seem to pay attention to the comments; they were busy setting out bowls of beans, rice, chicken *mole*, salsas and guacamole on a kitchen counter. Soon the friends lined up to fill their porcelain plates and headed out to sit, eat and drink. In this part of the city the house could be called a mansion—two floors, four bedrooms, a studio, a patio spread out in back and a gazebo by the flower garden. The guests spread out and the smell of *mole poblano* quickly mixed with the scent of night-blooming jasmine.

Hours later after everyone had finished eating, the artist and another man entered the living room, lifted the Homey, as they all called him, and returned him to his usual home in the corner. Briefly, a wrinkle—almost a frown—appeared on the hardened, terracotta brow.

"Weighs a ton," the friend said, leaning against the wall and catching his breath.

"If I could," the artist said, "I'd make one as big as the Statue of Liberty."

"I don't know, man . . . at least this size you can move him around."

"Bigger the better."

"Hmm. But why make so many?"

"It's a habit. The more I make of one thing, the better I get."

"Is this guy here your last one?"

"Actually, he was my first."

"Really?"

"Yeah. The others are really better."

"That's hard to believe."

"Gotta look close. The little guys have more detail, more life."

"If you say so. Yeah, sure."

Later, as the guests drifted onto the sofa chairs and floor cushions, two of the artist's friends began speaking loudly. "It's gotta come from the soul, know what I mean?"

"We back to that again?"

"Yeah, man, soul comes from family, from your roots. That's what makes art . . . uh, authentic. Then you've got some kind of movement."

"Bullshit. It's just a bunch of dudes calling themselves artists."

"Why you always gotta piss on things?"

"Not pissing. Just saying."

"Want another beer?"

"Yeah, all right."

Alone in his darkened corner, the Number One Homey shrugged and his shoulders seemed to sag. His expression grew weary, his ears tilted as if they were bored with the discussion. He had assumed a pose of dreamy indifference, hands loosely clasped behind his back, one leg casually set forward, his body slightly bent forward at the waist, his tongue hanging out one side of his mouth. Meanwhile, the guests were so busy with each other—torrents of words and laughs, all to a thumping beat—that the transformation went unnoticed.

"Good night," someone said, and the Homey lifted his head.

"Yeah, night."

"Thanks for everything."

"Want me to call a taxi?"

"Nah, I'm okay."

When all the guests had left and the artist and his wife had gone off to their bedroom, the big Homey stepped forward. His eyes roamed everywhere. Ashtrays brimmed over, gobs of beans, rice and bits of limp salad lay spread on the dining room table. He could hear spiders outside in the garden spinning webs, snails crossing the driveway pavement. He even imagined moonlight shining through the leaves and on the dew-covered grass.

With an easy effort he sauntered into the kitchen. Then he opened the refrigerator and took out a beer. After twisting off the cap he lifted the cold bottle to his thin lips and drank it all. Next he pulled out the covered pot of cold *menudo*. He was about to search the contents when he saw a plastic container of leftover ribs. For a long while he gnawed on a single bone, finally dropping it on the floor and licking his muzzle.

The Homey returned to the living room, pausing to give out a loud belch, then continued. The floor creaked under his weight. He stopped to listen. His ears stiffened and he seemed to sense movement in the room. He sniffed the air and peered into the semi-darkness.

There, from somewhere near the fireplace, came a faint chuckle. Again, only this time it was a distinct, tiny laugh, followed by other small voices laughing. Number One frowned and a long, slow, gravely growl rose from his throat.

"Something funny?" he asked.

After a moment he heard them again.

"Who do you think you are?" said a high-pitched voice coming from the shadows. "All puffed up like you're alive or something."

"You think you're human or what?" another voice added.

"Shut up!" The big dog shouted.

"*Oye, pendejo.* Statues stay in one place. You're not supposed to move."

"I said shut up!"

"You think you own the place?"

"All right," the Homey told his small-fry brethren. "I'm going to bust you guys all over the place."

A dapper figure with a wispy goatee emerged from the shadows. "You and who else?" he said. "We can move around too, and we've got you surrounded."

"So what?"

Suddenly, the diminutive statue Frisbeed a stiff corn tortilla at Goliath's crotch. The disk broke into pieces and scattered at the Homey's feet.

Another small figure in an orange jump suit stepped forward, a hammer raised menacingly in one hand. "Come on, *loco!* We're taking you down!"

For a moment, the Homey almost felt sorry for the puny challenger about to strike. It would be so easy to make *chorizo* of this little one.

"Drop it," he ordered.

When the hammer tilted backward, the Homey licked his muzzle once. He caught the hammer in mid-arc, then used it to smash his attacker to powder and bits of unglazed clay.

"Who's next?"

He scanned the nervous smiles around him. Slowly they began to retreat.

"Hey, man," one said, "relax. Just testing. Don't worry, nobody's gonna hurt you."

"Hurt *me?* That's funny. That's really funny. I'm not worried. Do I look worried. Why should I worry? I'm the best dog here. Look at me. Ever see muscles like these? And check this face. Perfect. Teeth like knives. And I'm fast . . . "

"Yeah, man, we believe you."

"You'll never see another homey like me. I'm the original, the only original he ever made."

"He made . . . me," a tentative voice said.

"Me too," another said.

"He made us all equal!" shouted the statue with the goatee.

"No way, *güey.* But I'm the first, I'm the best," the Homey said, stepping forward.

"Wait!" the goatee cried. "I won't say no more. You're the first, the one, the only."

That's when the Homey went crazy wild. He flung himself at the terrified creatures, arms swinging, feet kicking, teeth snapping into his little brothers. He smashed them to pieces, then furiously turned and faced the others hanging helplessly on the walls or propped on easels. He ripped into the figures, tore away the sketches, the painted oil canvases, flinging the wooden frames on the floor.

When he was finished, he was breathing heavily. With a smug expression, he surveyed the room, listening, waiting for another challenge, another giggle, another obscene finger. Finally he shrugged, removed a comb from his back pocket and calmly began smoothing his head of hair.

In the morning the artist raised his hungover head from the pillow. His wife was still asleep. During the night he had heard noises. Now that he thought about it, he remembered a strange dream about fighting dogs. He rubbed his eyes, swung his legs off the bed and staggered into the living in his black boxer shorts.

For a moment the artist was quiet. Then he pressed his hands to his temples and screamed. The one remaining oil of a gouged, laid-back Shepherd cruising in a chopped and lowered, vintage Chevy fell to the floor. In the master bedroom the artist's wife opened her eyes with a start, then felt the empty space beside her.

The Homey stood in his corner, motionless, trying hard not to smile, thinking, "the fool will never guess who did it."

"What happened?" the artist's wife asked, bracing herself in the doorway.

"I yelled."

"What's all this? Sweetie, what did you do?"

"Broke a few things."

"A few!"

"I got tired of the same old stuff."

The artist stepped over to the Homey and tickled him in the groin. Then he approached his wife, who was yawning and stretching one arm.

"I'll clean up," he said and pulled her toward the bedroom.

# A House on The Island

For most of the semester Elena Álvarez drove the class relentlessly, and in the remaining days only Nan and Ricardo remained, ready for the end. The young professor and poet had frightened all the others from the island.

*Is this what you want?*

*Yes.*

*Me?*

*Does it matter? Right now we're good for each other. We're far from everyone.*

*What are you staring at?*

*The birds. They're watching us. I can see their outlines through the leaves, and with a little sky behind. They see our flesh. Imagine if they could think.*

*You're not concentrating!*

*Yes, Ricardo, I am.*

*Well?*

*Well what?*

*I'm done.*

*That's okay. Just stay with me a little longer. Stay the way you are.*

The leeside of the island was quiet, warming. A breeze filtered over the palms that lined the upper edge of the strand, and the light-blue water inside the reef was smooth with crys-

tal glints of light. On the cove's white beach two figures slept
deeply.

Elena tapped the lectern with a pencil until they woke. As
usual she began the morning class in a grumpy mood and without her first taste of coffee. The wall clock showed six minutes
after the hour.

"Ricardo, would you close the door? There's too much
noise in the hallway."

Unlike most Spanish classes, Elena's were held just inside
the entrance to the Life Sciences Building, far away from the
Humanities. Hydra and starfish collected dust in open cases
under the windows.

"Can you open a few windows, too, Ricardo? The air's
stale."

Elena wore dark, fish-eyed glasses. She removed them and
shuffled back and forth across the sand, snapping impatiently
at the two flaccid expressions, one in the first row, the other
in the third. Her complexion was soap-clear and smooth
above the beige wool-knit dress, plain, severe. A small,
intense woman, she seldom relaxed her students until well
into the hour. Her wide hips turned, legs apart, feet planted,
she scrawled several lines of words on the board.

*Just stay with me a little longer. Stay the way you are.*

Finally an image struck Nan and she displayed it timidly.
"Since the bird is in free flight, maybe the poet is suggesting
he has no will either. Maybe the bird means . . . "

Ricardo (bored) and Elena (thinking of real birds) listened
from habit. "I think I see it now," Nan said. "The poet wants
to be free."

Elena sighed and, after a long pause, suggested they forget
the poem and explore the island.

"This end is deserted," she said. "My father and I were the only ones who used to come here. There's nobody for miles around. It might be fun to take a look."

Ricardo threw down his books, but Nan wanted to know where they were going.

"To my house," Elena replied.

Nan begged Ricardo to stay.

"Don't be a wuss," he told her.

"Don't go, don't leave me."

He kissed her lightly on the lips. "Come on, let's break the routine."

Nan shrugged. She hadn't stuck it out this long only to be dropped before the semester's end. Professor Álvarez had something special in mind.

"Wait a minute," Nan said, and she hurriedly applied shadow to her eyes, brushed her hair and rubbed her front teeth with tissue paper. Next, she straightened and patted down her skirt. After brushing off some grains of moist sand at the hem, she was ready.

"Hurry up!" Ricardo shouted.

Elena had kicked off her shoes and was moving into the shade.

Nan quickly dabbed her armpits with talcum.

"Hurry, goddamit!"

Nan had always perspired easily, so grooming and precautions came to her easily, which is probably why she won a beauty contest as a Rotary Club entry.

"Come on, girl! Okay, I'm going."

Nan trudged after him across the sand and onto firm ground.

"Here, grab my hand," he said.

Nan held on and daintily hopped over a fallen palm frond.

"She's crazy, you know. Why didn't she just take us over to the cafeteria for coffee? What do you bet we get lost."

"She knows her way."

"The hell she does. Look, she's already stuck."

Elena had tripped on a coconut but was up and moving before they could reach her. "Don't be afraid, you two!" their professor called back. "Just stay close behind. And bring the coconut. We'll eat it later."

Elena was glad the path still existed, though it was now covered with tree roots and grass. But she worried that it was unused. She turned and decided to wait for the two students.

When they caught up, she told them, "I always came this way. My father would bring me on Vicente, our one-eyed *burro*. Poor Vicente. A scorpion got his eye when my brother José, the retarded one, left Vicente alone in the forest. 'How do you punish a dumb child,' father said, and I answered, 'if it wasn't Vicente's eye, it might have been José's.' And he shrugged as if to say José could afford to lose an eye."

Elena spoke as the three rested on a fallen tree trunk. Termites and rot had gutted the core. Nan was busy slapping the insects on her legs, annoyed at the heat, her sweat and Elena's digressions.

Their teacher continued: "After that, Vicente was always falling into traps. He'd knock you over if you stood too close on his blind side. He was next to worthless, so my father gave him to me."

"Did we have to go this way?" Nan asked. "It looked much better along the coast. We'd find a clearing, then a trail. But here we're going to get lost and I have to make a nine o'clock seminar."

Ricardo remembered their first date. They had gone to a movie before finals and Nan was tense. He was late in calling

for her and they arrived at the theater ten minutes after the
film had begun.

"I don't want to see it," she said.

"Why not?"

"We missed the beginning. Then we'll have to sit and
watch the first part of the next showing."

"So let's skip the beginning. We can figure it out."

Ricardo said he had read about the film and would
describe the beginning for her, more or less, from what he
remembered.

"So what's happened?" she asked as they approached the
theater. "What have we missed?"

"I don't know. I lied."

"Lied?" She searched his face. "But why?"

"Nobody's going to test you. There's no quiz, Nan."

Nan kept silent throughout the movie, and Ricardo didn't
have to explain what might have happened in the beginning.

Eventually Elena turned and faced Nan. "If you want to go
another way, go on. There used to be an old man who lived
above the rocks at the south end of the beach. He had two
sons, fishermen, who were always looking for mischief when
the wind was down. There's hardly any wind today. Be careful
if you go that way."

"Will you go with me, Ricardo?"

"I'm a coward."

Elena smiled and moved away. The three began pushing
through thicker brush, once losing the path, backtracking and
starting over again. The low cover thinned out, the trees grew
taller and the sunlight barely poked through the dense roof of
leaves. The air turned cooler, the path darker. Elena led them
in silence. The house was at the top of a hill at the end of the
valley. She told them many islanders were conceived in the

forest. "My father made love to nearly all the young women on the island and probably half of them were brought here."

They stopped briefly to drink water from a stream. In her eagerness Nan forgot bacteria, parasites and diarrhea. She drank handfuls in gulps.

"It's safe," Elena said bluntly. "The excrement always went down the other side of the hill."

Slowly they climbed out of the forest and onto a sloping trail that rose gradually into a lower growth of bushes and more wooded, stiffer branches. The ground became drier. Behind them the steep-sided valley flattened in the distance, stopping sharply at the sea's edge.

Caught in the moment, focused on each step, Ricardo long ago stopped whistling. He was climbing the hills above the old Pasadena freeway, a polo-shirted kid with a stick for snakes. And at the summit, on a clear day, he would see the ocean.

Nan was now hiking barefoot, her soles punished by rocks and an occasional thorn. Her clothes choked her; they cut into her waist and wrapped tightly around her chest and arms. Out of the shade, her skin burned. Exhausted, she began to panic. They had left the coolness below but Elena seemed to ignore the change and picked up the pace. Of the two students, only Ricardo, his nicotined lungs heaving, doggedly kept up, determined not to lose her.

Nan shouted for Ricardo to stop. Delirious, she waved her arms about wildly, screaming that she wanted to go back. Men in the forest. Scorpions. Rapists.

"Come back!" she screamed, falling to the ground. "Where are you going?"

She cried in great sobs for a long while, begging Ricardo to help her. Then she grew quiet. She wished she knew the time, but she had left her watch on the beach in her backpack.

Thinking they had trapped her into staying behind, she stood and stumbled after them.

The trail dipped and Ricardo urged his aching muscles into a run. Then he walked for what seemed an hour. The shade came in patches from the few trees that hung over the tall yellow grass. Long ago he lost sight of Elena but found her wool knit dress thrown carelessly on a dead branch. He wrapped it around the coconut and carried it in the crook of one arm.

Elena saw him stagger into the small clearing where she lay on a bed of dark-green moss in the shade of a big, leafy tree.

"I'm over here, Ricardo."

He steered his body toward the tree, stopped and sank to his knees. Ricardo set the coconut and dress on the moss while he caught his breath. But he was still too tired to pretend casualness, staring hard at Elena's naked body, which was stretched before him like a gift. Her skin glistened and her long, black hair fell loosely to one side next to the tiny pile of crumpled underwear.

"Why did you run off like that?"

"Isn't it obvious?"

Suddenly, Elena's almost diaphanous whiteness moved. Ricardo flushed and turned his head. *Stay the way you are.*

"You know," she said, pointing a finger at his shirt, "naked is the best way to cool off."

Ricardo fidgeted with his buttons, and Elena helped him remove the shirt and the rest of his clothes. They were quiet as he touched her with tentative, respectful hands. Then she grasped his shoulders and jerked him to one side, leading him on top of her, guiding him, forcing him closer.

Nearby, Nan watched the two figures, their flesh now glistening.

"No," she thought, "this is not happening."

She had wandered crazily down the slope and had fallen just before entering the clearing. After crawling close, so close she could hear their breathing, she pulled at the moss with her hands and wrenched out great chunks with her fingers. She had not seen them until she had almost touched them.

"Is this what you want?"

"Yes," Elena said.

"You really want me?"

Nan watched Ricardo's back arch as he raised up on his arms.

"Does it matter? Right now we're fine for each other. No one's around. We're far away from all men."

Nan glanced around. Beyond the two bodies more trees and grass. The sky not as blue now. Afternoon blue. Pale, a few clouds. She turned, her fists tightened. Elena constantly moved under his weight.

"What are you staring at?" he said.

Elena was peering over his shoulder. "The birds," she said. "They're watching us. See their outlines in the sky? They're watching all this moving flesh. Imagine if they could think like us."

"Hey, concentrate."

"I am, Ricardo. I am."

Nan wept in silence. What could she do? What things could she say to that bitch? The story about the house ended here. No house, no goddamn house. Never was. What's her excuse? A poem. "Let's go to my house, Nan. No more class, Nan. I'll tell you about my father's island. And the music, the music, Nan. Did you understand it? Have some coconut. It's fresh. More rum? The record's ending. Could you turn it over, Nan? How's your drink, Ricardo? Finished yet?"

"Well," Ricardo said to Elena in the clearing.

"Well what?"

"I'm done. Were you?"

"Not really . . . but that's okay."

"It's been a while."

Nan heard them clearly: "Don't worry. Just stay with me a little longer. Stay the way you are."

Nan crawled away, hurt and limp. Elena had sensed her near. Throughout. And Ricardo had seen her briefly. Later he left Elena to search for Nan. As it grew dark he followed the stream to its mouth. There, Nan waved to him on the beach. Before returning by the trail she had circled the clearing, castigating herself, slapping at tree trunks and branches, once painfully falling into a thorny bush.

Ricardo stumbled across the darkened sand. As he drew near, Nan rubbed the late-afternoon chill from her bare arms. Neither of the two students would look closely at the other, nor would they touch. Without a word they slumped down in the first and third rows. Bitten, bodies sore and sunburned, they closed their books, looked at the wall clock and quietly counted the seconds to the end of class.

# The Castle

Lisa screamed and dropped the telephone receiver when a neighbor had told her that Carlos was out in the street playing with a tarantula. In seconds, she was running across the lawn. When she reached her son, she yanked him onto the sidewalk and gave him a swat on the butt. "If only your father were here," she muttered, wincing from the sciatica pain in her right leg.

The tarantula began jumping, not high, not far, but enough so that the curious kids backed away. A gangly, red-haired boy, taller than the other children, ran off, saying he would get a shovel.

Lisa gave Carlos a shove toward the house.

"*Idiota,*" she said. "It could've bit you."

"No, it wouldn't. It just wanted to get across the street."

Just then the red-haired boy returned in a pickup truck seated next to a freckle-faced man who looked like the boy's father. The man shouted for everyone to stay back and slowly drove over where the big insect was, though he missed on the first, noisy pass. Returning in reverse, the right-side tires hit their target with two squishing sounds. The fascinated group of kids, who had watched it all in silence, now erupted with Wows! Ooohs! and at least one Awesome! As for Carlos, when the pickup flattened the hairy mound, he squeezed his mother's hand and closed his eyes.

Then the red-haired boy got out of the truck and retrieved a square-end shovel from the back of the truck. He handed it to the man, who in one swift motion scraped the wet mess from the asphalt.

"Come on," Lisa said and led him into the house, down the hallway and to his room. His punishment was to stay in his room until she called him for lunch.

For a while, Carlos lay on his bed with his head under the pillow and thought how nice it would have been if the tarantula had lived. He'd still be pushing it across the street, letting it touch the stick, nudging it, coaxing it. He knew he would play until his mother's pain had stopped; then she would call him and they would eat lunch together.

In the kitchen, Lisa lit her cigarette with nervous hands. The room was stuffy and the reflection on the white table hurt her eyes. Removing her sunglasses from the apron pocket, she again begged her husband to return. A prisoner of war for three years, he knew nothing of the problems at home, the car accident, her sciatica, the hours on her feet at the beauty salon, the monotony and silence at home, the scares Carlos gave her, knew nothing of the effort to wake in the morning, to speak, to smile, to keep the house as it was, ready for his return. *Carlitos, your daddy went away but he'll be back. It won't be long. . .*

And to fill the emptiness, to make it seem her husband was gone for a few days, for only a few weeks or months, Lisa assumed nothing would change, not even Carlos. For almost a year she would not cut her son's hair. She let it grow long and curly, despite what the other children said. Then on the day she received the telegram that he was missing-in-action, she told Carlos she would cut his hair. She had him sit on a stool, put an apron around his neck and began to snip with a pair of scissors.

"Daddy wants you looking like a boy," she said, eventually collecting the hair that fell to the floor and placing it in a large manila envelope.

"When is he coming home?" Carlos asked.

"Soon," Lisa said. "Someday soon. Would you like to write him another letter? You can tell him all about your new teacher and about the picnic in the park."

Carlos nodded and watched his mother rub her eyes as if she were trying not to see something. Even then he sensed his father would not be home for a long time, if at all, since his and his mother's letters to him were never answered. But Lisa told Carlos that at least now she knew he was alive, not "killed in action," as some of the other mothers and wives learned of their men.

"I know he's alive now," she told her son. "He's a prisoner, I just know he is."

Lisa said she loved going to sleep because that's when she could look for his father and talk to him in her dreams.

It wasn't long before Carlos discovered he could look for his father in his own way. It was only a game but it was more fun than waiting for letters that never came.

Often after school he would find his mother in bed fully clothed, reading her books in the wan afternoon light. Or she would be pulling weeds by the oleander bushes that bordered the backyard. Or listening to her Mexican *ranchera* records in the cool darkness of the den, sometimes crying.

Carlos would take her hand and say, "He's coming home, he'll be back," remembering only the scent of his father's cologne, his adenoidal laugh, his soft, kinky-wool polo shirt.

"*M'ijito*, go take your nap," Lisa would say. "Maybe you'll dream of your daddy."

"Okay, I'll go take my nap," Carlos would say and skip off to his room, close the door and change into his hidden clothes. He called them his daddy clothes and he used them only when he went into the hills to look for his father. He would put the pillow, his football and pajamas under the blanket so she wouldn't notice he was gone; then he'd slip out the side door of his bedroom, close it quietly and tiptoe along the side of the house. Once on the sidewalk, he would head to the dead-end of the street and go up the trail to the structure at the top of the hill.

Today, a Saturday, not long after the tarantula had been killed, Carlos decided his mother would keep him in his room long after his naptime. It was his punishment. He opened the door slightly and peeked into the hallway. His mother was talking to someone but it wasn't telephone talk. Probably reading her diary out loud, most likely an account of the tarantula episode. The diaries, so far three of them, were for his father to read when he returned.

Carlos sat on the edge of the bed, knowing his father wouldn't have minded that he played with a big spider. His father liked spiders and snakes and dark places. He wouldn't have punished him.

He opened the blinds and felt the warm sunlight on his forearms. The roses were in bloom and he could smell the jasmine beneath the windowsill. His temples swelled, his skin grew tiny bumps like football leather and finally he decided to leave. Maybe she'd forget him, maybe she wouldn't call him until dinnertime.

He leaned into the dry wind as he rushed up the slope at the end of the block. Beyond the dead-end was an even steeper climb. He leaped over the weeds in the ditch and headed into the tall, yellow-brown grass. He hoped the others weren't there, especially the red-haired kid who chased him into the tunnel the first time he had gone to the castle. He remembered the tunnel had been cool and hollow-sounding. Later, when he found Sam, the old man said it was the best place to be on a hot day, although you had to be careful where you stepped. Animals bite only when you bother them. But Carlos didn't know that then; he only knew the redhead and the others were outside waiting for him. So he crept forward, following the shafts of light that came through the small windows of one wall.

"The devil's gonna get you!" one of them shouted into the darkness. "Gonna eat you!"

Another voice added: "Gonna eat you like an *enchilada!*"

And a third voice: "Come on back! We ain't going to hurt you."

The voices echoed, pushing him blindly, further into the tunnel, making him stand up and stumble. Then something ahead of him moved. Carlos stepped back, but the voices again pushed him. It seemed the boys were right behind him. "The devil's in there! Gonna get yoooou, yooou, you . . . "

At the end of the tunnel, when he could go no further and could only touch solid rock or concrete, he turned to the left. After moving forward for several minutes, stumbling twice on what felt like rocks in his path, he began to see straws of light ahead. As he got closer, he saw that there were jagged holes in the tunnel's roof. Now it was warmer and he could see fallen chunks of concrete and twisted metal rods on the floor.

The voices were gone. He continued to the end of the passage and again turned to the light, trailing one arm along the concrete wall. Feeling helpless in the darkness and thinking the boys were right about meeting the devil, he began to cry. That's when he tripped on something soft.

Falling forward, he heard a deep, raspy voice call out, "Who's that?"

Carlos came down hands first on the concrete. Then he felt a touch on his back.

"Speak up! Who are you?"

"Carlos."

"Carlos, eh?"

"Yes, sir."

"Well, Carlos, this ain't no sidewalk. This here's my bedroom. Actually, my bed chamber. And you don't come in without knocking first."

"Yes, sir."

"You don't have to say sir."

"Yes, sir. I mean, yes."

"And stop crying. Only babies cry. Now, what're ya here for?"

"Some boys were chasing me."

"Well, don't you worry about them. Nobody comes in here. They always stay up top. You wait here. They'll be going pretty soon."

"I gotta get home. My mom'll be looking for me."

"Let's go over where there's some light."

He led Carlos around another turn where the sunlight tipped his long white hair. Carlos drew back from the darkened face in the shadows, wondering if he was the devil.

"I'm Sam, king of this castle."

"King?"

"What did they tell you?"

"That . . . that you were the devil."

Sam laughed and said he'd rather be king of the hill than the devil. "They told you that so you wouldn't come in here."

Carlos could make out an old face with wrinkly skin and glints of curious eyes.

"Take my hand," Sam said.

Carlos held the long fingers, and the two began to walk.

"Watch your step. These rocks keep the marauders from coming in."

After a short distance, Sam pointed into the gloom to a shadowy stairway cluttered with twisted pieces of more concrete chunks.

"You go on up top," Sam said. "Make a run for it. And don't fall into no traps. I got them all over the castle roof."

For a moment Carlos was unable to move. Then he felt the old man's hand on his back.

"Only fools get caught, and you ain't no fool, Carlos. Get up there and show them you ain't afraid."

Carlos emerged from Sam's castle and escaped without the boys chasing him. Since then, he refused to cry.

That first summer, he and Sam would spend their brief afternoons together on the tower, on the battlements or on the courtyard wall, counting houses or cars, standing guard or planning defenses against attack. And Sam would use strange words: marauders, parapet, fortification, forage. Once Carlos found his friend in the East Dungeon, as Sam called it, peeling a grapefruit. Sam had just returned from a foraging expedition.

"Want some?" he asked.

"No, thanks."

"Amazing what the peasantry throws away."

"I'll get you some forage from my house."

Sam refused the offer, saying it wouldn't be right. "A king gives charity," he said, "he never gets it."

Soon Carlos was named the king's apprentice. In a brief ceremony witnessed only by a dun-colored rabbit below a rock-pile battlement, Sam pronounced the boy's new title with slow and lofty language: "I hereby present to you . . . the special office . . . of royal apprentice honoris . . . in per-pa-too-ee-tee."

Most of the time the lessons were fun and easy. The hard part was in seeing the same things the king saw. The gargoyles always hid and the gnomes seemed to appear only in dark places where all they did was giggle. The king would laugh and say you had to try looking for these creatures in a special way; you had to concentrate and maybe catch them off-guard. Carlos squinted, he shielded his eyes, he looked out of the corners of his eyes, he closed his eyes, he blinked. Finally he gave up and said he might have seen them.

The king's lectures began wherever they happened to be. "Do ya believe in dragons?" he said one afternoon while relieving himself against the outer castle wall. "Ain't no such thing, Carlos. That's only in fairy tales."

But the tigers, the marauders and an occasional black knight would visit the castle from time to time. For some reason the king would always forget his plans for defense and he and his apprentice would hurry to the arena stairs and descend into the cool safety of the bedchamber.

In the front yard one morning, Carlos asked his mother what the old place on the hill used to be. Lisa was lifting leaves with a rake to drop into a big wicker basket.

"Don't you go up there!"

Carlos knew she would say that and calmly observed, "It looks a little like a castle."

"You hear me? I've told you before."

"Don't worry."

Lisa dropped the rake. "It was going to be a country club . . . for movie stars, I think. But they ran out of money and stopped building it. Now help me put the leaves in the basket. When we're finished, maybe we'll go to the plunge. Would you like that?"

"Do country clubs have plunges?"

"Pools, they call them swimming pools."

Carlos looked up at the king's castle, thinking that's why the courtyard goes down at one end. But why a tunnel around the sides? Sam says the marauders use the arena to fight in . . . but how come I never see them? Maybe if I look through my fingers like he does, maybe next time I'll see them.

"Carlos! Don't just stand there. Put the leaves in the basket."

Once, as Carlos was stacking rocks along the open side of the courtyard, the king asked him if his mother knew about the castle.

"Does she know you're here?"

"She thinks I'm in bed taking my nap."

"Maybe ya oughta tell her."

"She wouldn't like that. She always thinks I'll get hurt, and my dad wouldn't like that when he comes back."

"Where is he?"

"In the war. He's a prisoner and he'll be back when it's over."

They were silent for a while, and then the king took a deep breath and tipped his imaginary crown to the boy. "Just remember, Carlos, ya always got your castle. Yeah, it's yours too . . . Hey, show me your house. Which one is it?"

"That one," Carlos said, pointing. "See, the white one on the corner."

"Got your own room?"

"Yeah, but I still gotta play in the garage. She says if I play inside the house, I'll mess things up for when my dad comes home."

"So listen to your mom."

≈ ≈

Now, as Carlos crawled up the hill over the dry earth and weeds, reaching for handholds, he heard voices. By the time he was nearing the castle wall, the voices became shouts but he couldn't make out the words. He looked below at the white house on the corner and hoped his mother wouldn't call him for lunch, that she would forget, that she wouldn't call him until dinnertime.

Loose clods of hardened dirt rolled between his legs, bouncing, disappearing into the tall grass. Again the voices. He searched the hillside, trying the many ways of seeing what he had not seen before. The wind, thick with heat and the smell of sage, beat down the grass to form waves and slick little eddies where rabbits and birds like to lie. He couldn't tell whether the voices were near or far, for the wind would bring them close and then suddenly push them away.

He reached the wall, climbed through a hole at one end and started up the stairs inside the Tower of Power, as he and the king called the main lookout. He heard the king shout—and he never shouted unless he was preparing for battle. Carlos had seen this once but it turned out to be a false alarm. There were no marauders scaling the walls, just a low-flying helicopter.

Crouching low, Carlos moved past the broken courtyard tiles and slipped through the Armory of rocks and club-like metal poles. He listened. The voices came from the arena. Suddenly, Carlos heard the king scream as if he'd been hurt. He shimmied up a water pipe to the flat top of the arena wall and crawled across to peek over the edge. In the far, deep-end corner was the figure of the king, squatting, hands over his eyes, before the redhead and four other boys. They were older than Carlos by several years and were jabbing Sam with sticks.

"Come on, you faker!" the redhead yelled. "Scare us now! Come on, you old wino!"

The boys laughed, and then picked up rocks and began to hit the gibbering target. Someone suggested they drop him from above. Sam then lifted himself on one knee. Another thrown rock just missed and the redhead turned and scanned the arena.

"Well, look who's here."

"Run, Carlos!" Sam shouted.

"Shut up!" the redhead ordered and let fly with a fist-size piece of concrete that struck the king on the chin.

"Hey, kid!" another boy yelled. "Come on down. Don't you want to hit the devil?"

"Leave him alone!" Carlos shouted. He stood and ran along the top of the arena, glaring down at the marauders. "Leave him alone!"

"Look who's giving orders," the redhead said, and the others laughed.

"Get out of here! This is our place!"

"Your place?"

"Get out!"

"Make us."

The redhead motioned to the other boys and before Carlos could duck, they all threw their rocks. Carlos fell back onto the concrete, shrieking and kicking his feet.

"Let's go," the redhead said. "We got him good."

"What about the old man?" one of the other attackers asked.

"Forget him," the redhead said, moving toward the arena's shallow end. "He's not worth the trouble."

As the boys ran off, Carlos remained on top of the castle wall, pitching from side to side, still kicking and screaming, thick blood spilling off his face like an egg with a broken yolk.

By the time Sam reached him, Carlos was whimpering.
"What happened, kid? Move your hand away . . . easy does it.
Oh, my."

The king kept up a soothing patter as he lifted his apprentice in his arms and hobbled down the stairs at the end of the
parapet. Outside, in the shadow of the castle, the stooped figure slowly made his way down the hill with his moaning, shiv-
ering burden. At the white house on the corner, the king
pressed the doorbell twice with his elbow. Looking at the boy's
trembling face, he noticed the blood in and around the sunken
socket was dry, the other eye shut but wet with tears.

"Go ahead and cry, boy," he whispered. "It's okay."

Lisa opened the door.

"Your boy's hurt," Sam said. He couldn't say more because
Lisa erupted in a long, terrified squeal.

Later, after the ambulance arrived, after Carlos had been
treated, bandaged and given a shot for his pain, after Lisa
heard what had happened and was telling police officers, the
king stepped close to the gurney and his little apprentice. He
patted a small, exposed hand.

Carlos opened his good eye and whispered, "I saw them."

"Yeah?"

"All of the them. I know them."

"Who?"

"The marauders."

The bony fingers curled around the hand and the king
gave a squeeze. Then it was time for Carlos and his mother to
be taken away, red lights blinking, siren rising to a hurtful
pitch. Among the curious neighbors gathered in front of the
house, King Sam, his grimy, sweat-stained T-shirt and baggy
trousers announcing his status, watched and listened. Then he
spoke, more to himself than to anyone in particular: "We'll get
'em, kid."

# The Boy Who Ate Himself

How or why it started no one knew. As a baby, Tom seemed normal. However, his mother recalls that he did have fainting spells. About once a month, maybe more, Tom would stamp his feet, raise his arms and hold his breath until his face paled and he fainted. When he revived he would be quieter but otherwise as normal as his two brothers. His mother vaguely remembers he fainted a few times after he was denied something she had promised him, something like a visit to the zoo, permission to play outside or a donut. Chocolate was his favorite.

Shortly after his fifth birthday he was taken to a doctor. The pediatrician carefully examined the boy and prescribed a mild sedative. One of the green, children's size capsules was to be taken at least half an hour before each possible denial. This solution seldom worked, his mother says, because she could never anticipate the times she would break her promises. After all, she had two other children who demanded her attention and she could not schedule her day to suit the whims of an oversensitive child.

A neighborhood *curandero*, or healer, finally provided the solution: three solid whacks on little Tom's rear anytime he would start his fainting routine. Two aborted spells and the boy was cured.

About this time he began biting his fingernails. At first his mother dismissed the habit as a temporary nuisance, much like the eldest son's bed-wetting or the youngest boy's nose picking. It seemed to her that Tom was practicing a kind of grooming, like brushing his teeth or combing his hair. She would be patient and it would pass. Even when she noticed Tom gnawing at the flesh around his nails, she did not become alarmed. "Patience," she reminded herself, "the habit will pass."

But it didn't—and Tom continued biting, gnawing, chewing.

By his eighth birthday, Tom was also a master of concealment. He never displayed his abilities in the presence of his mother, and since his father had left the family and remarried, he only had to hide from his brothers who sometimes teasingly called him Rata. At home he usually kept his hands hidden under his armpits, behind his back or clasped in such a way that his mother and the boys wouldn't stare at the raw, painful spots on his fingers, thumbs and knuckles.

His third-grade teacher didn't wait long until she mailed Tom's mother a reproachful note indicating that her son's voracious attention to his hands had caused his classmates to ostracize him. Furthermore, his incessant biting distracted the students during their quiet periods or when taking tests. Would she please curb her son? And if Tom did not stop his ratlike habit, the teacher said she would take up the problem with the principal.

First came the jalapeño chili treatment. Announcing that she hated to do it, she applied the mashed-up pepper and watched his raw flesh soak up the juice while he winced and began to tremble. Tom refused to cry or even whimper. The jalapeño swabbing continued for three days, and although he was temporarily denied his usual pleasure, he quickly grew used to the spicy flavor and the burning in his mouth.

"He got to like it so much that he'd beg me to rub the chili on his hands," she remembers. "I had to think of something else. I even tried iodine but it didn't work. And he never cried. This time, though, I couldn't stand it, watching him twitch like that."

Finally, in desperation, Tom's mother tried vinyl gloves as a remedy. She bought a box of extra-small, lime-green gloves and showed him how they were like a five-fingered balloon if you blew into them. Before putting them on his hands, she inflated one and he laughed. Then she let go of the puffed-up glove and it shot across the room, which prompted another laugh. Eventually, she carefully guided each of Tom's damaged digits into the gloves. Then she ran tape around the top of the gloves at the wrist, thinking it would discourage him from removing them. It didn't. As soon as she was gone, he'd rip them off and continue nibbling.

The teacher, along with the principal's approval, sent an ultimatum: either the biting stops or Tom will be transferred to a school for problem children. His mother reacted angrily, complaining to the principal that her son was being treated unfairly, even cruelly. In the end, she realized Tom showed no signs he was outgrowing his "disgusting tricks," as she now remembers calling his habit.

For a while she thought of taking him to the healer again but decided against such a visit because the result might be an even worse habit. Reluctantly, she gave in to the school's ultimatum, and Tom was accepted by the county's school for emotionally disturbed children.

After a thorough examination, both physical and mental, the school's psychiatrists admitted they had never encountered such a case and were uneasy about any possible treatment. They told his mother that he would be closely observed for a two-month period, after which time a definite prognosis would be made. She, Tom's brothers and other relatives could visit him only on Saturdays; if his condition improved, he would be released for weekend home visits.

Tom's mother appeared satisfied with the arrangement. Since she was unmarried and had to work as a grocery clerk while raising three rambunctious boys, she confesses she was relieved that the doctors would now watch the son who caused her such worry.

As the weeks passed, Tom increasingly missed home and playing with his brothers, the deprivation only raising his anxiety. He begged his mother to bring him his toys, none of which he could play with or use because of his damaged hands and because the school had forbidden the patients toys that could be used to hurt themselves or others. Swallowing objects was also a concern.

Tom retreated to his corner of the play yard; undistracted, he proceeded to bite with even greater enthusiasm. Not just his hands but by bending over and contorting his legs, he managed to feast on his feet as well. Soon he drew the attention of visiting medical students, who would come in groups to observe the frightened, uncommunicative child who would lie by the far wall for hours, performing his many maneuvers. He had become an unusual yet routine sight for all visitors in the facility.

In a way, Tom was the star attraction. The curiosity did not stem from his compulsive eating disorder; rather it came from the professional concern about his body's unusual defense against infection. No matter how dirty his flesh was—and many subsequent experiments proved this—the open wounds that covered his limbs would never become infected. Nor would he bleed as much as expected. These observations soon attracted medical attention throughout the world, and Tom was subjected to more and more examinations. In time, he was transferred to an isolation ward at the university medical center. Here the specialists could observe his progress at all hours, even while he gnawed at what he could reach in his sleep.

His blood, saliva, urine and all other body products were treated as precious laboratory specimens. Teams of research scientists worked in shifts to isolate his body's chemical and molecular properties, hoping to solve a riddle that might lead to cures for many infectious diseases.

Fortunately for Tom's mother, she was spared the pitiful sight of her son. He had removed all his fingers and toes, leaving only the scabby stumps of his knuckles. He was also starting to bite and strip skin from his lower arms, shins, knees and shoulders.

About this time, the doctors concluded he would soon kill himself. In vain they tried to halt his progress. They strapped him down, they bandaged and tied his hands and legs, and at one point they fitted him into a straitjacket. But these procedures only led to Tom's insomnia, refusal to eat and loss of weight, so they were forced to remove the restraints that held down his body.

Toward the end, Tom seemed to channel his hatred for his keepers, for their detached, business-like emotions, by hastening his feverish activity. During the last two days he did not stop biting and swallowing the tiny morsels of himself.

Perplexed by their impending failure to stop such a rare and unique case of autocannibalism, the medical team retaliated with scrupulous efficiency. Three attendants were by his side at all times. Every ten minutes, two of them would lift the naked figure off the plastic bed mat, while the third wiped away the puddle of blood drippings, urine, bits of flesh, tissue and scabs, all of which would be analyzed in the laboratory. An array of monitors kept track of his vital signs, while a tube inserted directly into his stomach enabled attendants to feed him liquid nourishment.

After almost six days of such attention, Tom died at 5:48 in the morning. His glistening, emaciated body was placed and sealed in a vinyl bag and taken away for an immediate autopsy. About noon, just before the lab technicians' lunch break, a doctor from the medical center called Tom's mother to inform her of his passing. He regretted that they were not able to stop her son's self-destruction nor discover the cause of Tom's ailment. "However," the doctor said, "you should know that we will cover all his medical expenses, including burial costs."

Tom's mother now says she was confused about her feelings when the doctor called that day. "I knew it was coming," she reveals in the interview on the first anniversary of his death. "But I was glad the little guy was finally at peace. . . . Sometimes I wonder if I caused his problem. My boys ask me why their brother was like he was, and I tell them I don't know why. Just to say he was born that way or he got off to a bad start—that's not enough . . . So a few days after he died, the head doctor calls me to see how I'm doing. I'm listening but I'm not really listening because I'm thinking about Tom and all this stuff he went through. And then I hear him say they'll pay for everything. I'd been worried about the finances and really down about that. But all of a sudden, it's like I woke up and felt normal. So I said thank you."

# The Interview

*Buenos días.* No, stupid, it's late. *Buenas tardes. Antonio Chávez a sus órdenes.* Smile. *Good afternoon. My name is Tony Chávez and I'm interviewing persons of Hispanic origin.*

He mumbled the words, toyed with them, rolled them around, bit their edges, mocked them with gestures, raised his voice, deepened his voice, finally whispered the greeting with a beggar's humility. He wiped his brow and wondered if this heat, dehydration and sunstroke were worth eight dollars per interview?

*Age . . . sex . . . marital status . . . occupation . . .* While walking with his three-ring notebook through the yellowed, weedy lot, he tried in vain to find some trace of saliva in his mouth. *Religion? Catholic . . . Protestant . . . Other . . . .* Smog clogged the air and his lungs tickled when he breathed. *Where were you born? Where were your parents born?* Nearby, the freeway trucks revved into higher gears, blasting him like giant dentist drills. The noise and heat wrenched his mind from his body, creased it, folded it, let it hang in the air like burnt tissue paper. His hair curled, singed at the ends. *You call yourself Mexican, Mexican American, Chicano, Latino, Hispanic, Salvadoran, Guatemalan, Honduran, Colombian, Cuban, Dominican, Puerto Rican . . . Other . . . Good afternoon. I'm Tony Chávez and I'm . . . I'm thirs . . . I'm thirsty.*

109

Chávez stopped to scratch his ankles; burs covered his socks. *Have you ever felt discriminated against? No . . . Seldom . . . Often . . . .* He raised himself, and his head floated somewhere above his shoulders. *What's your usual response? Fucking heat. Got to do this at night.*

The worn dirt path led him past a junked car and a rusty stove with its insides spilled out in the weeds. Looking ahead he saw two bare-chested men sitting on a mattress in the shade of a lopsided tree. Between them was a brown paper bag, twisted at the top. As Chávez approached, the thin man with a snake tattoo on his forearm looked up alertly.

"What you got, man?"

Chávez tightened his grip on the notebook.

"You give us a dollar and forty-five cents?" an older, fat man said. "See?" and he pulled out the empty bottle from the bag. "Port costs a dollar forty-five."

Chávez glanced at the street. The wood-frame houses looked uninhabited. Shades were drawn, a low, squat Impala pointed up the driveway, and a dog lay quietly by a shabby picket fence.

The tattoo leaned closer to the visitor. "What's your hurry, man? Sit down."

"I'm looking for ..." Chávez opened his notebook. "Tomás López. You know where he lives?"

"What you want him for?" the fat man said. "You don't look like no cop."

"I'm taking a survey and I want to talk to him."

"Talk to us. *A ver*, ask me a question. I've got all the answers."

"Leave him alone, Pete. He don't want to talk to no winos. *Mira*, he's all nervous."

"Hey, you think we're winos?" Pete raised himself slowly.

"I didn't say that."

"But you think we're winos, no?" He held up the bottle, then heaved it into the weeds. "Winos, huh?" For a moment his puffy eyelids closed.

Chávez waited, speechless, afraid of what the man's next move would be.

"Well, that's what we are. *¿Qué no*, Jess? Two goddamn winos trying to get the *feria* for a little juice." Pete scrutinized the newcomer. "Hey, man, we ain't gonna hurt you. Sit down."

Chávez steadied his voice. "Yeah, okay," he said and dropped heavily onto the mattress. The fat man remained standing.

"How about a little wine, man? You lend us something to buy a pint?"

Chávez removed his wallet from his pants pocket, slipped out a ten-dollar bill and handed it to Pete. "Get me a beer."

Jess reached for a shirt hanging from a low limb. "*Oye, buey*," he said, throwing it to Pete. "They won't let you in the store without a shirt."

Pete stretched the T-shirt over his wet belly and walked away through the weeds and down the hill.

Through the haze beyond the freeway, Chávez could see the outline of the Music Center buildings. He tried clearing his throat but the phlegm wouldn't rise. Closing his eyes, he felt the dark pit begin to close in. He began to walk in a circle and when he fell, the velvet lid or whatever was above him descended softly around his ears. Darkness was heavy, then it spoke: "Hey, man, you sick?"

Chávez opened his eyes. Clammy hands held his face and the thick smell of alcoholic sweat pricked his nostrils.

"What's the matter with you?" Jess asked.

"Huh?" Chávez rubbed his sweaty forehead with his free hand. His other arm still clutched the notebook. "I guess it's the sun, too much sun. I'll be all right."

Jess looked at him closely. "You go to school, don't you? That's why you can't take a little *pinche* sun. Man, you're in poor shape. That's what happens to you school guys. Shit, I used to pull twelve hours in the sun and all I got was a better sun tan."

Chávez sat up, notebook on his lap. *Macho, brags, likes sun.*

"You got that clean look. But you don't look too sharp now."

"Listen, how about if I interview you instead of Tomás López?"

Chávez opened the notebook. *One warm body is as good as the next. To hell with Tomás López. What do they expect for eight dollars an interview?* He stared down at the blank form. Once filled out, it would join hundreds of other forms to be classified, coded, scanned into computers, results studied and neatly presented to the public as a precise, up-to-date portrait of the Latino population in Los Angeles. *So big deal if Macho Jess here subbed for Tomás López. Big frigging deal.*

Jess gestured to the notebook. "What do you want to know?"

Chávez pushed down the top of his ballpoint pen. "Well, like your age."

"No! Don't write nothing down."

"But that's not how you do an interview. I ask you questions and then write down your answers."

"How do I know what you're writing?" Jess grabbed the binder and closed the cover. "Don't write nothing down."

"If it makes you feel any better, I don't even know your name."

"How do I know you don't? Come on, man, everybody knows me."

Chávez shrugged. "Okay, but I'm going to write it down anyway, later on. Now give me back the notebook."

"I'll give it back when I'm done talking. You just listen. I ain't as dumb as you think. Now what do you want me to say?"

"Everything . . . what you do, where you're from."

"Hm . . . well, like I was in the Navy, man."

### Navy veteran

"I ain't always been here. No way José. I got in the Navy when I was sixteen. No, really, I did. They sent me to Oakland. And you know what I did? I painted those big ships. Yeah, me."

### Occupation: painter

"I had some good times, man. Got to travel, see the world, got me this tattoo."

### Decorated

"But they kicked me out after I beat some *cabrón* over the head with a spray gun. I sprayed him good. He called me a little wetback. I can't take that from no one. So I sprayed him real good."

### Honorable discharge

"When I got back to El Paso I got married. And, man, that was the wrong thing to do. My old lady wanted everything. Like she wanted a new car. Man, I couldn't buy no new car."

### Low income

"So my *compa* and me went out and stole one. Yeah, jacked it right off the lot. Black Chevy. Wasn't really new but it smelled like the real deal. I knew she was gonna like it. So I dropped my *compa* off at his place, then drove over to show my wife. I tell her, but you know what she did? She called the cops. Now what kind of wife is that? I was just doing what she wanted."

### Adjusts well to environment

"I got two years in prison just for tryin' to make her happy."

### Thoughtful

"But guess what? After six months in the *bote*, they let me out. Said early parole for good behavior. Ha! All because I stayed outta fights."

### Good citizen

"Then I find out my wife's been seeing another guy. I blew up, smacked her, got my things and left. We got divorced and I never seen her since. That's how I got here. Never been back to El Paso. And I got another lady. See that house over there? The blue one? That's mine. I painted it myself. I got four kids. No, five. All of them boys. But they ain't like me. They're going to stay in school and be something, like you maybe.

### Five children
### Pushes education

"See, and you thought I was a bum, *puro* wino *nomás*, just sitting on my ass all day. Well, I got a family and a job and this is my day off. What do you say about that?"

Chávez noticed Pete shuffling toward them at the edge of the empty lot.

"You got more questions, Mister College?"

"A few more but I can skip it. Here comes my beer."

"No, go on. Ask me another question."

"Okay, what's your religion?"

"*Católico romano*, man."

**Catholic**

"Like I was gonna be a priest. Yeah, I was real close. But I joined the Navy instead."

Jess saw Pete coming along the path and he stood, turning his back to Chávez. A colorful Virgin of Guadalupe spread herself across his shoulder blades and ribs down to his waist.

**Devout**

"I had enough for a quart," Pete said excitedly.

"What about my beer?" Chávez asked.

"What's he saying, Jess?"

"He thinks you forgot his beer."

"Hey, that's right. I did forget. Sorry about that. But hey, don't worry. We'll give you some of our wine."

"No, thanks."

"You don't have to thank us. We didn't give you nothing."

"That's an understatement."

"Under *qué?*"

"Never mind."

"*Oye*, Jess," Pete said. "Let's go. The old lady says she's going to call the cops if we don't go."

"Who's that?" Chávez said, looking confused.

"Oh, the *vieja* in that old house," Pete said, motioning to the blue one.

Just then the curtains in a window moved.

"*Metichi vieja*, always after us."

"Isn't that where Jess lives?"

Pete smiled. "What's he been telling you? Shit, he ain't got no old lady."

Chávez looked at Jess. "But you said . . . "

"I said nothing."

"And the Navy and . . . "

"Sure, and my great-grandfather was Pancho Villa."

The two men started to walk away when Jess turned his head. "Hey, Mister College, Tomás López died two years ago."

Chávez wiped the sweat from around his eyes, picked up the notebook and hobbled out of the shade. "Wait," he yelled, trotting after the two laughing figures. "Let me have some of that wine!"

# Lupe

In the early morning, Tiburcio's wife Isabel gave birth to a nine-pound, eight-ounce hermaphrodite. Isabel immediately asked to see the yowling baby. She pushed up on both elbows, smiling, eyes alert. It had been her easiest birth, so easy that Cuca the midwife hardly did more than hold Isabel's hand.

Her pregnancy had almost gone unnoticed. To her other children she appeared the same, perhaps rounder, her eyes more affectionate. She had told them that one day soon their new brother or sister would arrive from her womb, clean and innocent—not "bought" at some mysterious store, as some of her neighbors liked to say.

Cuca hesitated, then held up the naked infant, its combination of boy and girl protruding before the mother's happy inspection. Isabel counted the fingers and toes.

"Any birthmarks?" she asked.

"No," the old woman said, raising a wrinkled brow.

"He looks like his father, wouldn't you say?"

"He, Isabel? It's just as much a he as a she."

"Then *she* looks like her father."

Isabel blinked and lay back on the pillow. Before she dozed off, she asked that Tiburcio and the children be allowed to see the baby. They had been waiting in the kitchen for more than an hour, and the pot of Quaker Oats that Isabel had been cooking was still on the burner, lumpy, cold and hardly mixed. The contractions had come so fast that calling the hospital was out of the question. Even Cuca—two blocks away—almost missed the event.

Tiburcio entered the sunlit room first. He patted the small, bald head, smiled and nodded to his wife. The eldest son Robert moved close and said all newborn babies look alike. Eventually the other children touched the tiny hands, made faces and wondered if the birth meant they didn't have to go to school that day.

"Go to school," Isabel whispered, closing her eyes.

Isabel was soon flooded with sympathy. Some called the baby a "he," others maintained it was a girl because of one very long strand of hair above the left ear. Other neighbors switched back and forth, sometimes saying the baby was very pretty, *muy chulo*, sometimes very pretty, *muy chula*.

"What about a name?" Tiburcio asked. "We just can't keep calling our new baby *it*."

Her husband was right, Isabel thought. "Any suggestions?"

No one spoke. Tiburcio nervously opened a telephone directory, his fingers flipping pages, eyes scanning up and down.

"Tiburcio," Isabel said, "go ask the priest. He should know."

Tiburcio jogged two blocks toward the river to the church and around the back to the sacristy. He found Father James and quickly explained the predicament. After a brief meditation on the matter, the young, Spanish priest shook his head, shrugged and advised him to pick a name before the baptism.

Cuca was more positive. There was only one solution: an operation. Afterward, naming the baby would not be a problem.

"Absolutely not!" Isabel cried. "No one's going to touch my baby."

In the afternoon, Fausto and his niece Carmela, neighbors from across the street, stopped by to congratulate Tiburcio and Isabel. The baby was asleep in its crib. Isabel was propped up with pillows, and Tiburcio, who was scribbling names on a pad and just as quickly crossing them out, explained the situation. Fausto, an old timer from Chihuahua, studied the baby, circling the crib and stroking the hairless crown of his own head.

"Well, what do you think?" Tiburcio said a bit nervously. "We need a name."

"Lower your voice," Isabel said. "You'll wake the baby."

"Well, Fausto? You're the man with all the books."

Carmela reminded them that her uncle wasn't a magician.

"Lupe," Fausto said. "Guadalupe. Either way it fits."

Tiburcio raised his heavy body and looked at his wife. "What do you think?"

"Fine," Isabel said and sighed.

She looked around the room at the smiles, then at the creature in her arms and suddenly realized the baby seemed to be smiling too.

"*Tío*," Carmela said, "I think we'd better go. You need your nap and Isabel has to rest."

"Sure. Now that Lupe has a name, a siesta sounds perfect to me."

Carmela kissed Isabel on the cheek. "You take care," she said and led her uncle out the door and through the living room.

The unopened presents were still piled on a table in one corner; the baby shower had been planned for today but Lupe had arrived two weeks early.

"Poor woman," Carmela said when they reached the sidewalk. "All those kids and one more to take care of. God, I'd hate to be in her place. She says her mother can't even help her."

"And why not?"

"She lives in Texas, and there's no money to bring her here."

"She'll survive. Isabel's a strong woman."

"Has to be. You see Tiburcio? He's like a walrus. She must spend all day cooking for him."

"He's nervous. Some people eat when they're nervous."

"All the time?"

Carmela steadied her uncle's arm as they crossed the street. "I'd be nervous too. Six kids, lousy job."

"That's why he's nervous. He lost his job."

The two entered Fausto's house. The old man sat down next to a bookcase jammed with paperbacks, magazines and hardcover discards from the county library.

"Carmela, that man is desperate. A strange baby's one thing, but giving it up to some circus?"

"You're kidding!"

"That's what he told me. What could I say? It's his kid."

Two days later, Tiburcio, with fear in his eyes, stumbled up the front porch stairs and banged on Fausto's door.

"*¿Qué pasa?*" Fausto said, flipping up the screen door latch.

"My kids, they won't eat."

"So? It happens."

"No, I mean a whole day and a half now. Nothing. All except for Lupe. He doesn't stop eating, nursing all the time."

The two men stepped into the kitchen. Fausto sat down at the table and turned on the antique radio. The cracked dial knob was loosely held together with a Band-Aid and kept slipping off the metal rod in the center.

"What'll I do?" Tiburcio said with a hapless expression.

Fausto finally stopped the dial on the station he wanted. The announcer was giving the day's astrology reading.

"Maybe," Fausto said, "your food is bad. Is that it?"

"I tried everything, even *capirotada*. They never turn that down."

Fausto leaned forward and listened for Sagittarius. After a moment, he looked up and told his sallow-faced friend not to worry. "You know children. They probably planned this weeks ago. On the other hand, it might be the weather. It does funny things. Or maybe they're like me. Sometimes I get tired of eating, can't stand anything—*todo me da asco*. You ever feel that way?"

Tiburcio slapped his paunch. "That's another thing. I haven't eaten all afternoon. It doesn't even bother me. Just not hungry."

"See what I mean?"

"What's crazy is I don't miss food."

"Tiburcio, go home, and I'll read up on this. Maybe I'll find an answer."

For two more days the children of Elysian Valley fasted. Then one by one the adults were afflicted by the same indifference to all forms of food. School was closed and some parents straggled to work for a few days. By Sunday only the strongest and most faithful of the St. Ann congregation were able to listen to the dark, weary figure seated on a stool behind the pulpit. By the fourth day, most of the children lay in bed with vague, limp expressions, their parents not much better. Even Fausto, searching his books, could barely stand any reference to food.

As for Lupe, the baby had quickly sucked his mother dry. Isabel was forced to fill the hungry little mouth with bottles of formula milk, watered-down coconut water and weak chicken broth. Hour after hour, Isabel trudged between the kitchen and the crib, stepping around her reduced husband, who was sprawled on a living room sofa chair. Occasionally, she stopped to rouse an eyelid of one of her other children, all lined up on a single bed like sardines.

It wasn't long before Lupe and his emaciated neighbors captured national attention. Reporters wandered freely through the homes, describing the scene of full cupboards and refrigerators, untouched freezers, blank faces and the usual skinny forms buried under bed sheets. Television crews marched in with their portable units, focused on pale cheeks, trying in vain to provoke a few intelligible words for their viewers. Nothing worked; they were left with silence or the continuous sucking and slurping sounds of one voracious, healthy infant.

"Fate," the Los Angeles mayor announced, "rests in the hands of medical intervention." The teams of doctors and nurses moved in with their machines, monitors, medicines and advice.

Most of the tests were run on baby Lupe. A hermaphrodite was unusual but, of course, not impossible. What was most strange was the baby's unceasing appetite. Medical professionals and other observers, now in white hazmat suits, could only admire such phenomenal digestive development.

By the second week the neighborhood had been placed under quarantine—in case the starving condition turned out to be contagious. Reserve troops from the Glendale Armory guarded all exits and entrances, while overhead two helicopters and several camera-equipped drones watched for anything suspicious, especially along the riverbank on one side and the Elysian Park hills on the other.

About this time, Fausto lifted his eyes from a worm-eaten page, crawled past a dozing Carmela to the front door and feebly shouted, "I know! I know!"

A male nurse stationed outside stared through the rusty screen at the decrepit figure on the floor. "You say something?"

"Yes," Fausto cried. "Take me to the baby's house."

"Okay, but they're not going to let you in."

The young man then carried Fausto across the street to Tiburcio's house. The soldiers, reporters and medical people gathered on the lawn looked like a rookery of beakless, all-white penguins.

"Hold on!" a soldier shouted to the nurse carrying Fausto, who was dressed in blue, flannel pajamas. "You can't take him in there."

Fausto wagged a bony finger at the Plexiglas panel of the hooded soldier. "I know something . . . important," Fausto said.

The soldier hesitated, glanced at a nearby, nodding doctor and gestured with his rifle to the front door.

A television cameraman hoisted his camera onto his right shoulder. "Hey, Trish," he called to a slight figure at the curb who was checking her phone screen. "The old man!"

By the time the cameraman pointed his lens in the right direction, it was too late: Fausto had disappeared into Tiburcio's house.

Inside, the nurse set Fausto down on a chair. "Get me a banana," he said to the medical team.

"What?" one of the hazmats asked.

"A banana," Fausto repeated. "A ripe one, not green."

"What did he say?"

"Said he wants a ripe banana."

"So get him a banana."

"Right, a yellow banana."

Upstairs, Fausto found Tiburcio lying in bed under a sheet and two blankets. Tiburcio's eyes were closed and his hands were folded over his once great belly. Fausto shook his friend by the shoulder.

"Shh," a voice said, "he's going to say something."

"Fred, get the lights on this."

"Hey, quiet!"

"Dammit, get the lights on."

"Shhh!"

"Make room, cable comin' through!"

"Make room yourself."

"Shut up, you guys. The old man's trying to speak."

The room turned quiet. "Bring the baby," Fausto said, "and the banana."

After Lupe was brought in, Fausto had him placed beside his father on the blanket. Tiburcio smiled at his chubby bedmate.

Fausto now placed Tiburcio's hand on the baby's stomach. "Watch," Fausto said, moving the hand to Tiburcio's mouth. "First it goes in the mouth, then you chew it, then you swallow it, then it goes down to your stomach." Fausto slowly repeated the words and motions.

After the third lesson, Fausto took the banana, peeled it and gave some to the baby. Tiburcio watched Lupe open and swallow his first bit of solid food.

"Now, do the same," Fausto instructed, nudging the rounded top of the fruit between his friend's quivering lips. The cavernous eyes blinked twice. Tiburcio bit down. "Yes," his eyes seemed to say, "the taste of a banana."

The crowd of hooded penguins cheered, cameras clicked and one broadcast reporter snatched up the banana peel to dangle before the lens, then held a microphone to Fausto's face.

"Could you tell our viewers what you did, Mister?"

"Tejada, Fausto Tejada."

"Mister Fajada, what exactly did you do?"

Fausto, now eating a banana himself, swallowed, cleared his throat and took a swig of water from a plastic bottle. "It's a remedy for curses and lost appetites," he said. "It's the fruit of Capricorn, the goat . . . "

The reporter frowned and waited a moment longer. "Is that it? A banana?"

"A ripe one," Fausto said with a mischievous scan of the expectant gazes behind all the rectangular, Plexiglas face masks. "The Tarahumaras of Chihuahua believe that goats eat everything—grass, leaves, flowers, *hierbas* . . . "

"What?"

"Herbs!" a Chicano cableman shouted from the back of the room.

"What did he say?"

"Bananas and herbs."

"Louder!"

"Bananas and herbs!"

Fausto raised a hand and waited for the crowd to quiet down. "If you want a cure for the mysterious," he said, addressing the camera, "you eat some . . . you know, whatever's on the ground. But I knew Tiburcio wouldn't eat *that*, so I gave him a banana, like the horoscope says. Actually one book said goats really only like the leaves of banana and plantain plants. But they get by on all the rest because most of them don't live in the tropics. So they make do."

He nodded and smiled when he saw Tiburcio guiding a bottle of water to his mouth.

"Bananas? The leaves? Mister Fachardo, you can't be serious."

"I am."

"You expect us to believe this is a cure? Bananas? Really?"

"Why not? It works for my friend. Try giving some to the baby's mother. You'll see. She needs it the most, poor thing."

Just then, another cordless microphone weaseled its way between two hazmatted figures. A shrill but muffled voice asked, "Mister Fajada! What if a person's allergic to bananas? Or doesn't like the taste? What then?"

"I don't know."

"You don't know?"

"No, ma'am. Look, I know I was taking a chance, *pero más vale ser caprichudo que mudo.*"

"English, please, Mister Tejardo."

The cableman in back was laughing, then he shouted, "It's an old saying! It goes something like . . . uh . . . it's better to take a chance on . . . a banana . . . than to be silent."

"That it?"

"Well, in Spanish it rhymes."

"Okay," another reporter said, "but what are you saying, what does it mean?"

"Don't be afraid of taking chances," Fausto said. "And you better do it soon—before it's too late."

"See to it," a deep voice ordered. "Immediately."

"Yessir!"

Tiburcio, cradling the baby, tugged at Fausto's sleeve and whispered, "Ask them if they've got anything else to eat."

Tiburcio got whatever he wanted and very soon everyone else did too. Donations from all over the country poured in for the hungry people of Elysian Valley. Most everyone had breathed on death, had even touched death, but fortunately there were no unhappy endings.

Months later, when the ordeal was over, a proud Tiburcio could be seen parading around his newest offspring, swearing that—rumors to the contrary—his little Lupe would never work in a circus.

# The Story Machine

That summer they discovered him by the river playing his old tape recorder to the weeds and dry rocks along the lower bank. His mouth was like Henry's mother's mouth, turned down at the ends. His thick eyebrows, hair flaring out at the edges, looked like Tina's father's eyebrows. The man's wobbly saucer ears were those of Carmela's uncle's ears. And he had the smooth, muscled arms of Raul's stepfather.

The children stepped closer, at first hesitantly, then eagerly, to stare at this man with his machine and his green dog, the big spools of tape going around and around.

They hardly noticed the dog, which besides its bright color was scrawny and had sunken, lazy eyes. Henry Mendoza, oldest of the four children, asked the man what he was doing with the machine

"Playing stories . . . Listen."

The children sat down on the sloping concrete and waited.

"How come it stopped?" Henry asked.

The man glanced at the top of the river bank. "It's better if we go over to the middle of the river."

Tina shook her head. "My mom says I can't go in the river."

"It's dry," the tape recorder announced, its spools slowly turning round and round. "Nothing will happen to you."

"There's still some quicksand," Carmela said, ignoring the machine. "Last year a boy died in the quicksand."

"Nothing will happen," the machine said in a louder voice. "I promise."

"Why's he green?" Raúl asked, pointing to the dog.

"Is that you talking in the machine?" Henry said.

"How do you do it?" Tina added, wrinkling her nose.

"No more questions until we move," the man said, and he rose like a tired bedspring, lifted the machine by the handle and went off toward the dry river bed. The dog scratched its ribs with a hind foot and waited for the children to follow.

"All right," the man said after they had gathered on a sandbar, "who wants to hear the first story?"

Four hands went up.

"Who was first?"

"Me!" they all shrieked.

"Let's start with the youngest first. What's your name?"

"Raúl."

"Okay, Raulito. This one's for you."

The machine spoke but this time it was Raúl's voice.

*Tina's father is mad. She forgot to empty the wastebasket and he punished her. She has to stand in the corner of the kitchen for a long time. Now she sees an ant crawling near the dirty dishes. She asks the ant to take her place so she can play in the sink. The ant says okay, and Tina gets down like an ant and starts to play. It's a lot of fun because she can slide down the knife with the butter, jump in the cranberry sauce, do a somersault into the spaghetti and skim across the dishwater on a tortilla chip.*

The three children listening to Raúl's voice on the machine turned to look at their little companion. He was silent for a moment and then he smiled, feeling a little proud. "Now it's Carmela's turn!" he said excitedly.

Carmela blushed and her cheeks turned the color of an apricot's ripe, reddish side.

The man never touched the machine, and the reels of magnetic tape slowly kept turning. When the contraption began to speak with Carmela's voice, which was very deep for a girl, the dog raised its ears and flicked its tail once.

*Henry wants to be a frog and hop around the house. But he doesn't know how to be a frog. His mother is always sad and he wants to make her laugh. Finally he meets a big frog, a giant frog with green, bumpy skin. Can I borrow your skin, Henry asks, and the frog says, here, but don't take too long, it's all I've got. When Henry goes up to his mother, at first she thinks he's a frog. Then she sees his socks are inside out, and she starts to laugh.*

The children laughed, too, and even more when the man's green dog began to hop over the sandbar making sounds like a frog.

Then it was Tina's turn. The machine spoke with her small, squeaky voice: *Raúl asked his stepfather if he would like to have a real son, not just a stepson. But his father wouldn't answer. Right away they went to see the monkeys at the zoo. For a long time, Raúl said, you think I'm a monkey. And his father tickled him on his throat and made funny noises the way monkeys sometimes do.*

After a long yawn, the dog put its head in Carmela's lap and completely relaxed under the soft strokes along its back.

It was Henry's turn.

*Carmela's Tío Fausto is always bringing home bums and winos. One time he brought a lady who looked lost. She also looked very poor because she had holes in her sweater. Fausto gave her food, then drove her to where she lived under the bridge. Everyone knew she was bad, and Fausto even let her steal the clock that was on the television. Later on, he said he was glad she didn't take the TV too.*

"I have to go now," the man said, switching off the machine. "I'll see you tomorrow."

Carmela petted the dog's green hair once more. Then it trotted after the man who climbed up the concrete slope and disappeared over the top.

"That was neat," Henry said, breaking the silence.

The others nodded slowly like grownups, then ran across the sand, over the gravel and back to their homes.

The stories were not kept secret. The four children told everyone about the man and his machine. Their parents smiled or asked silly questions or said something about not speaking to strangers. No one really worried. They were just kid stories.

But the stories came true. The next day Tina's father punished her and she played on the dirty dishes.

Henry forgot to take off his socks, and his mother laughed.

And because it was Saturday, Raúl went to the zoo with his father, heading straight for the monkey cages.

Even Carmela's story about her uncle and the lady came true. Only she didn't take the clock. Instead it was a bar of Dial soap and an old bottle of her aunt's perfume.

Every afternoon the children went to the river. The man seemed to like it there, but he would always leave in a hurry as soon as the machine finished its stories. The only thing he told them was never to follow him and his dog. And they never did, mostly because they didn't want him to get mad and maybe go away for good.

Even though the stories came true, the older people still weren't too curious about the stranger with the story machine. After all, they were harmless stories, something that made their children happy.

But one day Carmela's voice spoke from the machine and said that Henry's older sister had died in a car accident. Henry felt like crying when he heard the words.

When the children went home, as usual they repeated their stories. Henry choked when he came to the end of his. Soon the prediction spread throughout the neighborhood, and his older sister was locked in her room in case there was some truth to the story.

Parents were furious. Tina's father rounded up neighbors to follow him like a posse behind the sheriff. They were going to find the stranger—and who knew what they would do to him? The four children tagged behind, hoping their friend would not be found.

After a long search, the posse discovered the stranger and fell on him like a flock of crows. He had been sitting with his machine and green dog, quietly chewing a carrot among the tumbleweeds under the freeway bridge. Before they could reach him and his barking companion, he turned to the crowd and hesitated, as if waiting for the children to catch up and go with him. Then he jerked to his feet and sprinted away with the dog. He seemed to fly, barely touching the ground, over the far bank, quickly losing himself among the freight yard trains on the Glendale side of the river.

Henry's mother found the machine, which in his hurry the man appeared to have forgotten. She raised it high in the air and flung it hard on the concrete. Then she tore the plastic tape into crinkled, spaghetti-like strips.

Hardly anyone slept that night. Many were thinking Henry's sister would somehow escape from her bedroom, drive away in the family car and die in an accident. But the next day came and went, and nothing happened to her. She even confessed that on the night that the story predicted she would die, she had slipped out a window to go see her boyfriend in Griffith Park.

Since the accident story never came true, the Elysian Valley parents were relieved, some of them hoping that the stranger might return with a new machine to amuse their kids. But the four who found the man with the green dog remained in a funk for weeks. Then gradually, little by little, they remembered and began to tell and listen to their own stories.

# Acknowledgements

**A House On The Island**—*Revista Chicano-Riqueña: A Decade of Hispanic Literature, An Anniversary Anthology*. Houston: Arte Público Press, 1982.

**Awakening**—first published in this short story collection.

**Bedbugs**—first version published with the title "Chinches," in *Latin American Literary Review* 5/10 (Spring-Summer 1977).

**The Boy Who Ate Himself**—*Quarry West* (1980).

**Canine Cool**—Original version published as "Perros" in *Caracol* 2/ 4 (1975).

**The Castle**—*Bilingual Review* 3/2 (May-August 1976).

**The Chamizal Express**—*Open Places* 37 (Spring/Summer 1984).

**Eddie**—first published in this short story collection.

**El Mago**—*El Grito: A Journal of Contemporary Mexican-American Thought* 3/3 (Spring 1970).

**The Interview**—*Revista Chicano-Riqueña* 2/1 (Invierno 1974).

**Lupe**—*Cuentos Chicanos: A Short Story Anthology*. Revised edition. Eds. Rudolfo A. Anaya and Antonio Márquez. Albuquerque: University of New Mexico Press, 1984.

**Stoop Labor**—*Revista Chicano-Riqueña* 2/1 (Invierno 1974).

**Story Machine**—*Revista Chicano-Riqueña: A Decade of Hispanic Literature, An Anniversary Anthology*. Houston: Arte Público Press, 1982.

**The Wetback**—original versions published as a chapter in the novel *The Road to Tamazunchale* (Reno, NV: West Coast Poetry Review Press, 1975) and in *First Chicano Literary Prize 1974-1975*, Department of Spanish and Portuguese, University of California, Irvine, 1975.

# ALSO BY RON ARIAS

*The Road to Tamazunchale*

*Five Against the Sea*

*Moving Target: A Memoir of Pursuit*

*Healing from the Heart* (with Dr. Mehmet Oz and Lisa Oz)

*White's Rules: Saving Our Youth One Kid at a Time*
(with Paul D. White)

*My Life as a Pencil* (a chapbook)